BLACK HOLE

BLACK

HOLE

BUCKY SINISTER

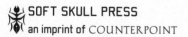
SOFT SKULL PRESS
an imprint of COUNTERPOINT

This book is a work of fiction. Names, characters, places, and incidents either are
products of the author's imagination or are used fictitiously. Any resemblance to actual
events or locales or persons, living or dead, is entirely coincidental.

Library of Congress Cataloging-in-Publication Data

Sinister, Bucky, 1969-
Black hole : a novel / Bucky Sinister.
pages ; cm
ISBN 978-1-59376-607-8 (softcover)
1. Drug addicts--Fiction. I. Title.
PS3569.I5757B58 2015
813'.54--dc23
2014044580

Cover Design by Matt Dorfman
Interior design by Sabrina Plomitallo-González, Neuwirth & Associates

Soft Skull Press
An Imprint of COUNTERPOINT
2560 Ninth Street, Suite 318
Berkeley, CA 94710
www.softskull.com

Printed in the United States of America
Distributed by Publishers Group West

10 9 8 7 6 5 4 3 2 1

For Alex Morris. I miss you every day.

BLACK HOLE

THEN ONE DAY, you're the creepy old guy with the drugs. That guy. Fuck. I used to talk so much shit about that guy. When did I become him? One day your friends think it's funny that you get fucked up and throw up everywhere, and the next day they're having an intervention for you. Drugs start out as a social event, but in the end, you do drugs alone.

There's something romantic about being young and strung out. Even when you look like shit, you kinda look good, and there are drug buddies your same age and you get high and come down and get high again and you don't know what day it is and you talk about plans and life and you confess all the horrible shit that's happened to you to someone you met at a bar on Friday night and it must be Tuesday, and shit, we're almost out again, do you know anyone who can get us more, do you have any money, cuz I'm broke, I'm broken, I bent myself so badly I can't ever be straight again, I'm a human wire hanger you used to get your car unlocked and here's all the things we should do together because we'd be the best team and we're going to accomplish our hopes and dreams and fuck everyone else, you're the best friend I've ever had and we'll never be alone again.

But then you catch your reflection, and you're the freak in the corner of some party where everyone's half your age. Sure, it's cool that you're there, you brought your own drugs and your shit's so much better than what they usually have, but someone asks you what the '90s were like, and you're telling them about the Pearl Jam Nirvana Red Hot Chili Peppers New Year's show that you blew off because it was too mainstream, and someone else tells you that was the year they were born, and everyone looks at each other and laughs.

I would love to get off this shit, get off everything, and be some square who goes to work and goes home and does whatever those fucks do when they're at home. I would love to have a beer and watch TV in my mancave. You know, normal. Those fuckers who have a drink at the bar and go home. Who smoke pot once a year at a wedding. Who go to bed early because they have work the next day. Who are dull but don't mind. And that's the part of it I can't wrap my mind around: the DULLNESS of it all. But with the dullness, the chaos would go away.

It's the chaos that fucks with me. The drugs, I like, but the bullshit of finding them and paying for them, and some tweaked-out dude freaking out on me, the calls in the middle of the night, the weirdos knocking on my window—all that shit I could do without. Unless you have movie-star money, chaos always comes with the drugs. And if you have movie-star money, you won't have money for long. The drugs will take as much as you have and return only a habit.

I'm forty-three. Own nothing to speak of. I sublet a room in a rent-controlled apartment. I have a bank account that's a little more than a high-tech mattress I stuff my money in until the first. It rarely has more than a month's worth in it. Sometimes I have to deposit a few bucks in to get a twenty out.

San Francisco used to be the town where you went if you were a weirdo with no money, and the Mission was the home for those with even less than the others. The Lower Haight was the cool place to live, and if you couldn't afford it there, you ended up in the Mission. There was a small lesbian enclave there before they all moved to Bernal Heights and Glen Park and bought houses. There were a few Irish bars still there from back when it was an Irish neighborhood, way back before World War II. Other than that, it was a Latino neighborhood when I got here. People just offhandedly call it Mexican, but it's a wide representation of Central America and some of South America.

Every day, I come out of my place and look at what's happened to the neighborhood. There's been riots and gangs and drugs, but the worst enemy the neighborhood ever had was money. If you think it's about race or class or crime, you're wrong; it's only about money. It looks like dope or crack or pussy or tech, but it's always about money. Every broken car window and every asshole coding away at Ritual Coffee Roasters is about money.

The money didn't start with the tech market or the dot-com game. The money's always been a part of this neighborhood, pushing it, propelling it. The corners for drugs, the alleys for prostitution, the pawn shops, the SROs, the porn—it's all money. Money ran this neighborhood then, and the only thing that stopped that money was newer, different, bigger money, much bigger money: tech.

It started with biotech, quietly, a little bit of money coming in here and there, then the dot-com days came and Eggers set up his trophy charity on Valencia, a place for Marin moms to drop off the kids while they went to trendy brunch spots with the girls, and slowly the thrift stores became vintage stores and antique stores and no one complained when there was a new police station with a rock garden with Good Vibrations across the street and there was another tapas place and a yoga studio and things got expensive but hey, the dot-coms folded and everyone breathed a sigh of relief, but it was only a few more years until the real tech companies showed up and things went batshit.

So one year it's *vatos* by the payphones and a few years later, it's the techies on their cell phones, but they all use the neighborhood for money. Whether you're trying to corner a drug market or market a drug company, you've come to the right place. So now it looks like I'm talking about drugs, but if you know anything, the drugs are only a vehicle for money.

There's still a little bit of the old neighborhood here. It's hard to see unless you look in the right places, and those right places are often the wrong places—you'll see the truth but you'd better duck, you'd better hide because the truth is some scary shit you don't really want to see.

Just a few years ago, a Mongol shot a Hells Angel on Twenty-fourth. Then somehow the Sureños got involved and the Norteños jumped in and there was all kinds of shit going down. Seven people got shot before the cops arrested everyone they could and let them fight it out in county. This was all a block away from the artisanal ice cream shop, the place where you stand in line to get a basil pesto ice cream in a sea salt cone.

Someday the scariness of the neighborhood will be gone, which is incomprehensible. They'll do to the Mission what they did to Times Square. Someday Seventeenth and Mission won't smell like an old tire filled with pee; someday the corner stores selling crack pipes and dollar cups of vodka will be gone and all the SRO hotels will be condos. I can't picture it from here, but it's going to happen. You'll walk by a yoga studio and some old fuck like me will be like, *That used to be the Irish bar where they found half a skeleton when they took out the drywall, and they never found the top half,* or you'll buy a Coach handbag where nothing used to cost more than a dollar.

I'm walking between the two worlds: the square world and the drug world. I go to work every day in the square world and spend the rest of the time in the drug world. I'll never have peace until I'm all the way in one or the other.

Took too much. Fuck. Again. Maybe if I just stuck to one drug at a time. Maybe I could manage that.

Last night, happy hour: drinks, more drinks, another bar, a bump of coke in the men's room, more drinks, that girl with the Vicodin. More drinks, a full line of coke in the men's room. Left the bar, went to a club. Did some new shit: remote. More drinks, more coke. A psychedelic drug too new for a name, a test batch fresh out of the Berkeley drug labs. That's a lot for one night. Maybe it was two.

Remote is fun, for slowing down or speeding up your perception of time. It's great with smoking speed or crack. It's fantastic for fucking, for that moment right before you come when you think your whole life leading up to this point was a great idea, but it's fucking hell on the crash when you can't control the speed. When someone else is holding your biological remote and just mashing the fuck out of it.

It was developed as a combat drug, to allow soldiers to remain calm and slow down firefights in their minds. Didn't really work. Actually, a slowed-down firefight is much more frightening than a high-speed one. That's why your brain does that, makes it seem like everything happened so fast.

But you know all those great moments that never last? That instant right before orgasm, especially? You can slow those down and wallow in them. Remote is the best thing to happen to sex and drugs and rock and roll since ecstasy. It works great in conjunction with other drugs, and since I'm always on other drugs, I go through a lot of this shit.

With remote and DMT, you can spend what feels like days of being high during the actual shortness of your lunch break. At remote parties, the DJ spins music sped up to incredibly high rates, indecipherable to the sober, but you can listen to entire catalogs of artists in only minutes, real time.

The only real problem is coming down. Time slows when you're detoxing. You can get so slow it feels like endless pause. You can be stuck wherever you are, alone with your thoughts, and god fucking help you if you're in pain at the moment or staring at the sun. What looks like just a second to everyone else can feel like weeks or months. The boredom will drive you insane. People's minds pop on this shit. There's even rumors of total pause, where you're perceptively stuck forever. It's a paradox that makes my brain hurt just thinking about it.

Sidewalk is ankle-deep wet mud. Moving in slow motion. Tenderloin, heading up Jones Street, and I don't know why. Don't remember how I got here or what I was doing.

A centipede of Vietnamese ladies runs for the bus down the hill, opposite my direction. I'm a drugsick rock in the middle of a stream. I'm losing ground, being pushed backward. These women with their pink plastic bags mean business.

A refrigerator-sized skinhead sees me from across the street. His eyes widen. This isn't paranoia; this isn't the coke crash talking, drug psychosis; this is the real shit. He's real, and he's coming for me, wading through a sea of old women.

His head is a peppermint of knuckle-white and sunburnt-red. Black button eyes sewn into his face. Cable-cover veins run up the side of his neck and spread across his temple. Smoke coming out of his collar, swirling off the top of his head.

My hand in my pocket. A .25-caliber Raven. Yes, my little popgun. When did I get this? Have I always had it? He's getting all six: five in the clip, one from the chamber. That's if it's loaded at all.

Fearsweat and sickness. Slog up Jones Street, but it's slower as it goes.

He gets closer in quick jumps, like a movie with missing frames. He's a slideshow of impending doom. He's going to stomp me out, kick me with steel-toed boots, grind me between heel and sidewalk. I don't want my teeth crushed. Everything else heals. Teeth are fucked forever.

Wait until he's close enough to read the tats on his neck. Grab him and jam this ridiculously small gun in one of the few soft spots he has—right underneath the sternum and between the top two ab muscles, these tiny lead pieces will take the fight right out of him. I'll take my chances with the law but not with this hulking monster. You can still smoke a motherfucker in the TL.

The uphill sidewalk steepens. It looks like a fucking wall covered in cigarette butts and blacked circles of old gum. I can't move. Too sick. Guts clench; I'm falling to the ground.

A hand constricts on my arm, tightens with a grip like a blood pressure machine. Bicep about to blow out. I can't move the arm. Can't reach the Raven with the other. I'm fucked.

CHUCK, he says. He knows me. I look in his face. I know this guy from somewhere. He's sweating from the top of his head.

His veins pulse like an equalizer light with a Godsmack song on. Big Mike. It's fucking Big Mike. Isn't it?

Big Mike? I ask.

Yeah, bro, who else would it be? What's up with you? You okay?

Sick. Jonesing. Hurting bad.

That's why they call it JONES STREET, bro! Come back with me, I'll get you right.

Back in the day, Big Mike and I dated dancers that worked at the same club. He was a Cal lineman back then, but he lost his scholarship for a buffet of reasons. Academic failure. Legal trouble. General scariness. Gridiron mayhem. Too violent for football, you know, spearing and shit. Using his helmet as a weapon. Going for the injury instead of the tackle. He was a goon, someone coaches only wanted to have in order to injure other specific players. He had the mean streak and the strength, but with none of the subtlety; Big Mike was as flamboyant about hurting someone on purpose as a pro wrestler.

We were two losers with stripper girlfriends, getting high and killing time while they were at work. He was out of a scholarship, and I couldn't hold a job. Behind every stripper is a man wasting her money. They make it from men and take it from men, but usually they spend it on some other fucked-up man, a man who is well more fucked up than anyone they're getting money from.

Big Mike talks the whole way to his place, but I can't follow it. The sickness turns his voice into sad trombone music. I'm fading fast.

●

At the bottom of the stairs, he tries to talk to me, but it's no good. He alters his speech to make something listenable, but there's no hope. Garbled shit, I can't understand a thing.

He picks me up like a sack of laundry and carries me up the stairs. People walk by us in the hallway, but it's that kind of building in that kind of neighborhood, where if you're carrying a body to your place, no one will say shit.

He lays me down on a mattress. I watch a fly above me. It pauses midair. I'm so fucked. Even if he comes back for me, I could be stuck like this, staring at a fly forever. Five minutes go by; the fly moves again.

Big Mike returns with various drugs, holding them in my line of vision. Crack, no. Heroin, no. Speed, no. Remote, yes. Please. Fuck. Please. I try to speak, but nothing comes out. Something registers though; he saw the look in my eye.

He dips an eyedropper into the vial and holds it out over my eye. I see the drop form on the tip, and it pauses there. Fuck. Not now. Not here. Don't make me wait. I can't get stuck like this. I stay like this for seven, eight minutes, staring at that drop before it finally falls from the dropper.

Everything comes back.

We're in a studio apartment that smells like cat food and burnt plastic. My eyes sting. He's hotboxing crack in here.

You feeling it? he says, leaning over me.

Yes.

This shit is hella scary, bro.

You don't have to tell me.

I mean, it's great, until you get a habit.

Really, you don't have to tell me. The sickness is worse than any-thing. You just freeze wherever you are, stuck in time. In reality it's not happening, but it feels like you can be stuck somewhere for days. Maddening.

I look around. Mirrors are haphazardly placed around on all the walls, like whatever he found thrown out he hung up. They're dirty, chipped, and cracked, and they don't all reflect the same image. The only furniture in the place is the mattress I'm on and a squat rack with a bench. Weight plates lean against every wall. There's a garbage bag full of empty tuna cans.

Haven't seen you around the clubs, he says.

Nah, got a straight job. Takes up too much time.

You? Straight job? What are you doing?

MiniWhale.

What the fuck is that?

We make dwarf whales for rich fucks.

Shut up.

No, really, every rich fucker wants his own whale right now. All those startup guys and software nerds have one. And the Russian gangsters are crazy for them. They're like an Italian supercar, you know, something most guys buy just because someone else they know got one and they can't have it.

How much do those cost?

Hundred grand to get started.

People buy those?

Bro, there's a waiting list.

So what are you doing drugsick in the TL if you have such a good hustle?

I'm just cleaning the tanks; I'm not getting a cut.

You got a lady?

No.

You got money?

Fuck no.

You want to put in some work for me?

Is it legal?

Big Mike busts up laughing. *Bro,* he says, *you are fucking hilarious.*

THE TRUTH ABOUT MINIWHALES

EVERY YUPPIE AND techie wants his own Moby Dick whale. And why wouldn't they? There's no cooler whale; until we get the killer whales or narwhals, it won't even be close. Blue whales come in a distant second. Way far in the back of the pod is the non-albino sperm whale.

But all these fuckwads have to have one. And if you want one, we're the only game in town. You can get them from us, or you can settle for last year's dwarf goats with their inner-ear problems and their shit-spraying assholes. You can get the dwarfed bison with their rage flare-ups and their bad pelvises.

If you want a MiniWhale, you have to come to us. We trademarked this shit. Sure, someone else will make a tiny swordfish or some shit, but if you want to be a whale, you have to own a whale.

If you're going to be taken seriously, you need a condo south of Market with a Tesla in the garage and a MiniWhale tank in the living room. You don't know what a thread count really is, but your sheets have the best thread count possible. Your bathroom has heated floors, and your kitchen has more stainless steel than RoboCop. There's no evidence that you were a scrawny nerd in high school, and you prominently display your CrossFit medals and your Tough Mudder participation trophies.

The whale tanks are as common as giant Macs and ugly furniture. You have to have a sixty-inch TV, some kind of unusual coffee maker, and a whale tank. Pets are the new accessories. They're the killer app; they're the brand-new status-power cocktail; they're the newest electric car. Accessories, all of them. No one wants things because they want them; they want things to show the world what they can afford. If you spent the hundred grand that a Roadster cost in 2010 on Tesla stock, it would be worth over a million bucks now, but no one would be able to see you drive your stock portfolio down Market Street.

Here is the dirty secret: the Moby Dicks are clones. Here's the problem with that: the more we clone them, the crazier they get. Like insane crazy. Like serial-killer crazy. It's like making a copy of a copy or something. We're cloning off an original sample, but there's still some kind of mental deterioration.

We sell them as unique dwarf breeds straight from the ocean. Each one is supposed to be different, but they're all the same. Not exactly the same, as they're technically a little worse each time. I don't get it; I'm not the fucking whale scientist.

Eirean, my boss, is the one who got rich off this. I won't. There's always stories you hear about someone who was an original Yahoo employee or some shit, not even one of the engineers, just a receptionist or something, who is now worth a shitload of money. It was the big chase of the first dot-com wave and is happening again in the tech age of San Francisco. No one's getting rich except a few lucky dickheads.

I clean the tanks. I feed the whales. I transfer the whales to the van. I deliver the whales to rich fucks in the mirror-walled condos that rise like giant glass dicks south of Market. I build their tanks and balance their water and remove the dead whales when the rich fucks are too dumb or stupid to feed the poor whales right or they piss in the tank during a party or something.

I'm a grunt. I'm working at the bottom of a high-end company. I can't afford to take home what I work with all day. I can't afford one of these whales. I know them better than anyone, and I'll never own one.

If it weren't for rent control, I wouldn't be able to live in San Francisco anymore. It's all software guys and biotech people, app developers, and big pharma. It's weird how big it's gotten here. The dot-com bust was supposed to end all this shit, and it's bigger now than it ever was then. And unfortunately, it's also a lot more stable. These companies have actual revenue streams. Some of them will go away, but a few of them never will. They'll turn into AT&T or Pepsi or whatever of whatever it is they do. In the end, all these app companies will be owned by two big companies, and no one will remember when there were thousands of little ones like these.

Someday, these will be the shit jobs with the glut of employees that are overqualified and underpaid. Until then, though, if you have a software engineering degree and a beard, you're a rich motherfucker sitting in the techbird seat.

Of course, without these rich fucks, no one would be able to afford these whales, which would mean I would be out of a job. I'd be back to living off girlfriends and sleeping on couches. Honestly though, I might have been better off back then, as far as general well-being goes. Those were happy times, even though I was depressed through most of it. I only enjoy that era in retrospect. Should've been the best time of my life.

If you're in your twenties and not having a great time, you're fucking up. It's never going to be that easy for you again. You're going to fuck the hottest people in your life, and it's not going to be difficult. You're going to get drunk and the hangover won't be that bad, and you're going to get high for days and it won't really matter. When you're twenty-two and you pass out at a friend's house, it's totally normal. When you do it at forty-two, you're never invited back.

In my twenties, I lived in San Francisco when you could still get by working part-time. My rent was always about two fifty a month for a shared room in a flat. I worked at a newsstand, a couple of cafes, and some bars. I often had anywhere from three to five jobs that were each one day or so a week. I hated working anywhere more than twice a week.

The slacker years. Gen X. Grunge. All that shit I hated being said about me and us. You told me I was grunge then, I would've told you to fuck off. I was punk. But, looking back at the pictures, yeah, it looked more grunge than punk. But still, we hated all that shit being shoved down our throats.

Now I'm well into my forties, and I have no idea what the fuck I'm doing. Drugs are more of a juggling act. Druggling. I have to get right more than I get high anymore. Trying to keep it at normal. I rarely enjoy being loaded nowadays. It's another job. Work a job all day, then work a job all night. Stay right.

Until I figure it out, I'll be right here, arm-deep in a dwarfed whale tank. Cleaning the tanks, feeding brine shrimp to some, krill and plankton to others, this weird whale chow that's supposed to be what they have in the ocean. Fuck it, they'll eat anything. What's the problem? Is it going to stunt their growth?

THE WORKOUT

BIG MIKE DOESN'T go to a gym; he lives in one. He has a squat rack, a bench, and a rack of dumbbells in his studio apartment, weight plates and mirrors lining the walls. No room for a bed. Rarely needs a bed. When it's time for his body to rest, he takes some GHB and sacks out on a bare twin mattress on the floor.

Powerlifters and true bodybuilders are rare sights at gyms these days. When you do see them, it's like spotting a white buffalo in the wild. It's not the skinny little guys being made fun of at the gym; it's the guy who has the bloodstream of a chemistry set and the veins you can see running down his arms. The giant freaks have disappeared like dinosaurs.

Gyms aren't for lifters anymore. They're for people who want to lose some weight, not pack it on. Guys want their arms to look better in a shirt at the bar, and women want to sweat off water weight and see that magical weightporn number on the scale. Juice bars and Zumba classes. There are gyms where you can't dead lift, for fuck's sake.

And forget it if you're really hardcore, like Big Mike. No place is okay with juicing. You can't shoot a syringe full of roids in a locker room anymore. And it's not just roids for Big Mike. It's crack. Big Mike smokes crack and lifts. Just smokes and lifts and lifts and lifts. Bench presses like a piston. I lose count of the reps.

How many do you do?

To failure, he gasps. *I don't count reps anymore. If you're counting reps, you're not serious about it. It's about the pump, the failure. If you can lift more, you're not done. Then you add or subtract weight, and you do it again. And again. Three sets of twelve are for assholes at the chain gyms.*

He sets the bar, gets up, puts these two-and-a-half-pound weights that look like CDs in his hands on either side of the bar.

He's wearing black boxer briefs, a tank top that looks like two strings hanging right over his nipples, and nothing else other than a body full of faded prison tats, all skulls and snakes and a bunch of scary gang shit I don't want to know about. He's probably butt naked when I'm not around.

With every movement, muscles fire and relax. Veins pop, just below his skin, scattered across his arms and face like a roadmap. His whole body reddens.

When his muscles finally fail, he stands back up, and there's a noticeable shift in his sweat slime as it rolls over his prison ink. There's a look on his face that's a mix of euphoria and befuddlement, like he just got a blowjob from a ghost.

He methodically opens a can of tuna and eats it in a couple of fork scoops. He throws the can at the trash bag on the floor, drinks a ridiculous amount of water, then picks up the glass stem and hits it. He extends it to me. I wave it off. He shrugs and gets back under the bar.

We have to get moving soon, I tell him. *I can't keep the whale truck all day.*

Last set, he says. *I gotta get a pump. Help yourself to some stash. Any speed?*

I have a little bit of everything. Look in the kitchen.

The kitchen is a haphazard mess of street drugs and workout supplements. The cabinets are populated by bags of weed in eighth-ounce bags. A fire-hydrant-sized tub of Mass Blaster.

Oxy. Creatine. Ecstasy. Nitric oxide. Vicodin. Glutamine. Percocet. Beta-alanine. What is this shit? 714s? Those can't be real. Fake ludes. He wouldn't have real ludes up here with all the riffraff . . . Dexedrine. Yes.

There it is. Fuck this Adderall shit; Dexy is my pharmaceutical speed of choice. I pop one in my mouth and take three for later.

There's more in the fridge, he yells. *Mostly roids and T, though.*

I'm taking two Dexys. Is that cool?

Yeah, no sweat.

What should I take for later? What's the best thing in here for a speed crash?

More speed, he says.

SIZE MATTERS

BIG MIKE'S WEIGHT tilts the truck when he gets in. He's a massive man. It's not just the muscles; it's the neckless pumpkin head, the thick, fat-fingered hands. There's a difference between tall and big, but this guy is both at the same time.

He eats a microphone-sized protein bar like it's a job, methodically taking bites, chewing, and swallowing. There's no joy in eating among bodybuilders. It's only fuel for a constantly draining tank. Anyone else would have fun eating six thousand calories a day. Anyone else would die in a year from eating this much.

We're driving out to the racetrack in Berkeley. I always forget there's a track out here. Once a year or so I'll drive by it and think, I should really go there sometime, but I never do. Have a Bukowski day at the track, lay down a few bets, and drink some beers in the sun that only exists in the East Bay and never in San Francisco.

I've been up all night working the midnight-to-eight shift at MiniWhale, but the Dexys are treating me right. Pharmaceutical-grade speed is so nice. All the up and the pep without that teeth-grinding, fist-clenching tweakiness. This is the real shit. That street shit is garbage. Absolute trash. There are so many different better drugs to do than that. If you're doing street speed, you're doing drugs wrong.

It's been a long time since I crashed without the help of something else. Naked. That's how it feels. Coming down without the right drugs is like walking out your front door naked. You should take something to either numb out or amp up. And I'm not talking about taking some downers and passing out in a corner.

I need to really crash free of everything, let my body squeegee the bloodstream clean and start over. There's so much bullshit in my system that I can't tell when I'm high or crashing until it gets really bad.

Big Mike sniffs around.

Bro, he says, *crack a window. You smell like a cat peed on you.*

Yeah, I know, I say. *There's some gnarly shit we use to clean the whale tanks. I wash it off, but it gets in my pores and the speed is wringing it out of me. I think everyone at work is numb to the smell. They don't notice.*

Bro. I notice. That's the problem. I don't give a fuck what your coworkers think. This cab isn't that big.

So tell me, I say, rolling down the window and changing the subject, *when did all this giant skinhead stuff happen? I mean, you were always big, but this is ridiculous.*

San Quentin. I got busted bringing back a truck of roids over the Mexican border. With my record, I wasn't sure if I was getting out. That's when I got real about lifting though. I did all my time just eating, sleeping, and working out. It's not enough to be big in there. You have to be big and scary, and the skinhead thing was good for that. But it grew on me. I like it.

Big Mike stuffs the rest of the protein bar in his mouth like a shovel of coal going into a furnace. Even his chewing and swallowing is aggressive. Then he continues:

Scary is good. Scary works. Scary is better than a gun. If you're not scary, people will fuck with you so that you have to fight them or fuck them up or shoot them. If you're scary, you don't have to bother with any of that shit. They will find someone else to fuck with.

The sad irony of it is, some people get big for protection from others, but the roids fuck with their heads so much, they start fucking with everyone else. Roid rage is real, bro.

I knew this dude who got so jacked on roids he tried to fight a truck. He was going bananas with his sets, running around the gym after them, and we told him to run outside, so he'd get done with a set and run out the emergency exit, across the street, touch the wall of the parking garage, and run back. Well, one of the times, on the run back, he stops in the middle of the street, winds up, Popeye-style, and tries to punch this delivery truck as it slams on its breaks. Truck won. The truck always wins.

We pull in behind the racetrack through a service entrance. Fresh-cut grass and horseshit. Big Mike tells me to wait with the truck and wanders off somewhere.

I can hear the cars from the highway far in the distance. One of the places I lived when I was a kid was right next to a freeway. The sound of traffic always calms me. It's like the ocean for most people, I guess.

Someone tests the loudspeaker. It turns on with an electric pop, followed by a feedback wail and the words *TESTING, TESTING, ONE, TWO, THREE.*

I turn on KALX. I'm hardly ever out in the East Bay, but I still love picking up this station. They're playing Op Ivy. Fuck. Op Ivy. "Junkie's Runnin' Dry." Figures.

May 1989: I hopped in a van and came up here with Don and Tim. For no real reason, you know, just for the fuck of it. Among other things, we were set on going to Gilman. Op Ivy was playing that night. Of course, I got way too wasted and passed out in the van. Missed the show of my life.

But that's how I got here. When they went back, I just stayed. Fuck, it seems like yesterday. What the fuck happened? I'm over twice the age now that I was then. Old. Fucking old guy.

Back then, life was as long as you needed it to be. Days were just full of all the hours you'd ever want or need; they just went on and on, and there was time enough to do anything you wanted. Most days, I woke up with no idea of what I was going to do. No plans or responsibilities. And suddenly, the days click off much faster than you want them to, and you have to think about what year it is because it all moves through you without you noticing. You're busy as fuck even when your life is a zero.

And shit mattered. It just doesn't now. I used to think a good show would fix whatever was wrong, and I'll be damned if it didn't feel that way. Now there's nothing to get excited about or to look forward to. Shows happen, and if I do hear about them, they're already over, but what the fuck would an old man like me be doing at a punk show, anyway?

I crank it up, but it doesn't sound as loud as it used to.

Big Mike bangs on the door. Startles me.

Open the back, bro.

I get out, come around the truck, and don't know how to process what I see: a dead horse on a forklift.

No, no, no. I can't have a fucking dead horse in here.

What? Bro, don't sweat it. I needed your truck because it has the rear climate control. We have to keep this cold until we get where we're going.

Where are we taking it?

A butcher. I know a guy.

PARTY

I'M IN THE glow of a red light, I think I'm in someone's house, but I'm not sure. There's so many people around me that we're all touching a little bit. There's a girl looking up at me with big eyes, and she won't stop smiling. I'm screaming something at her that she likes over the music that's coming from somewhere . . . I think there's a DJ, but I don't see one . . . it's a mashup of the theme from *Footloose* and the James Gang's "Funk 49" with a thumping bassline . . . people are doing what is intended as dancing, but there's not enough room in here to do much else other than move up and down a little.

Right now, there's a party going on that you're not invited to. You don't know about it. You're doing whatever it is you do with your day. You're making a sandwich or looking for the remote or breaking up with your girlfriend or applying for another job while you're the job that you hate. But somewhere in the world, there's a party going on, and people are getting fucked up. Somewhere in the world, someone is having a great time, and you're sucking on a big ball of shit.

Hopefully, I'm at that party. I'm at some of these parties—as many as I can find. Parties are where I found out about drugs and sex and the best music I've ever heard. Parties were the place where I wanted to be me for the first time, where I was glad I was me and not someone else.

The best punk shows I ever saw were at parties, in an Oakland backyard, a San Francisco warehouse, or a basement in Olympia.

No one taped them, or filmed them. They're gone, in the air, living in the memory of thirty or forty people who saw the show. I think back to some of those shows, remember the friends who were there who have since died. Every so often, that show will live in one less mind. When everyone who was there has died, that show will no longer exist.

Now those bands are gone. I don't hear good bands anymore. I'm flooded with DJs with records and laptops, and yes, there are still bands, but they just feel like they're playing dress up; they look like throwback bands and cover bands, a copy of a copy of a copy, losing integrity with each generation. Or they look too perfect, punk bands with every spike carefully planned and placed. The old bands are getting back together to play shows that are full of twenty-one-year-olds who missed it the first time and forty-two-year-olds who want it to be back for one night, driving the minivan in from the burbs, old dads in young skater clothes.

What's left for an old punk-rock washout like me who doesn't give a shit about punk bands anymore? Drugs. Which probably means I was always more of a drug addict than a punk. I would tell you then that I was going to change the world with my ideals and a pair of steel-toed boots, but really, I wanted to get really high and listen to something loud and fast. Acid, Robitussin, and cheap vodka: a perfect cocktail for punk. But the drugs now are better than ever.

There are drugs you don't know about unless you're someone like me. For every drug that gets known enough to have a name, there are a hundred others that don't make the cut. There's a whole scene of indie-rock drugs too cool for a name that are fighting for their place in the market. But unlike the arts, this shit is a meritocracy. The best drugs will win, because it's not based on anything but how they satiate the horrible hunger of the drug addict.

There are drugs like Halloween stores that pop up and go away before you ever try them. Most of them aren't any good, but they're new, so people take them and get bored with them. The point is, there are too many for the DEA to give a shit about all of them, and until some suburban brats die taking them, no one will ever give a shit.

For every meth lab in San Bernardino County, there's an organic chemist in Berkeley making something new. What's the point of a new drug, some might ask. Well, if the drug just barely exists, there's no test for it. So for all the airline pilots and UPS drivers and parolees, they can take as many new drugs as they want because they can't test positive for something there's no test for.

In some tiny warehouse right now, groups of ravers take remote and a DJ plays audio and video at such high speeds you can't tell it's music and videos without being geeked out of your mind. They play *The Wizard of Oz* on the big screen with a dubstep remix of *The Dark Side of the Moon* compressed into seven minutes. They watch entire runs of *30 Rock* and *Law & Order*; they listen to the catalog of the Beatles and endless bootlegs of the Black Crowes. Richard Pryor routines lie on top of Miles Davis and John Coltrane records.

In another warehouse across town, everyone takes Multi, and DJs play multiple records at a time. To the sober, it sounds like a cacophony. On one hit, you can separate two sources of input. On two hits, you can hear four sources. On three hits, eight. And so on. Kids with hacked iPods walk home listening to several podcasts and all the Led Zeppelin albums at the same time.

On a floor covered in rubber gym mats, everyone lies still and leaves his or her body on a full hit of Astral. You watch the whole scene floating just underneath the ceiling while hearing the sounds of whatever's playing distorted by the astral fields, which makes Slayer sound like Enya. You can listen to Napalm Death, and it's the most relaxing smooth jazz you've ever heard.

And there are endless amounts of amphetamines, psychedelics, and downers that you've never heard of and never will unless you know some degenerate drug addict like me. By the time the media hears about them, they're gone. By the time they report on the scourge that's killing your kids, there's a new drug killing your kids.

If you're really into drugs, you're taking them before they have a name, before anyone really knows what they do, how long they last, how addictive they are. That's when they're good. Once they get popular, they're copied by chem labs in China that will reverse engineer anything you give them, and the knockoff recipe is made. It's never that easy though. The knockoffs are never quite as good as the real thing.

If you remember how you got to the party, you're not taking enough. You should feel like your existence begins and ends within the time zone of the party. There's no tomorrow or yesterday; your friends are the people right in front of you; you have no job other than enjoying yourself.

The power goes out. Everyone screams. The girl I'm dancing with pulls in close, wraps her arms around me. It's pitch black, but I'm seeing bright green Spirograph patterns like a screen saver in front of me. There's music from another part of the building, somewhere close, thumping in time with my heart.

A smartphone goes up in the air, lights up, and dubstep blasts out. The dancing starts again. More phones turn on, synced to the same phone and blinking a lightshow for us.

The girl I'm dancing with fingers my lips. I part them. She puts a tiny Tic Tac–sized pill on my tongue. I try to swallow, it but it dissolves into a bitter chalk powder. I hope it's good.

HOME

I'M ON MY way home after most people have left for work, walking on autopilot from the club. Sobering cool wet air, that thick San Francisco mist. I have blisters on my feet, my joints are electrified, and my jawline is sore. My throat is swollen with a killer thirst going on.

There's a box with newspapers. I get close enough to figure out what day it is. Monday. I'm working later tonight. If I crash out at home, I may not wake up in time. I feel like I'll really be out for a day or two. The only option is to take enough speed to get through work and come home after that. Keep this shit rolling.

Home is where your drugs are.

I put the key in and turn the knob.

A dog barks at me. I don't recognize this dog. New dog? Chihuahua, much like the other one. Do we have a different dog or two dogs? Or did I forget the one we had? It's beige attitude and tiny teeth. It barks at me all the way to the kitchen.

I can barely see the refrigerator from the amount of Post-it notes on it. They're all to me. There's arrows from one to another, to bills that I owe on. I open the door. If any of this food is mine, I don't remember which is what is whose. Fuck it. I grab the milk and chug it. I'm so gakked out I can't tell if it has gone bad or not. Even if it has, I'm much worse than the milk. Immediately, it swirls in my stomach. I don't know if it will last in there.

The smell I don't recognize is me. I smell like smoke and old beer and my own personal BO. Shower is needed. What, since Friday? Yeah, I'm overdue.

In the bathroom, I start the water, lock the door, and empty out my pockets. Wallet. Keys. A bindle of some new dance-club amphetamine that just came out. A tin of mints, with nothing but four Vicodins. A vial of remote. A scrap of paper with a number and name smeared with sweat so it's unreadable.

My T-shirt is dirty, like I was rolling in the fucking alley or something. Hella gross. My shoes come off, and my feet throb. Under my socks, they're red and swollen and there's a matching set of blisters on each one. The pants are getting loose; my underwear comes off and a blast of ball funk hits me. I think I might have fucked someone this weekend.

I squeeze a drop of remote out and get in the shower. The first blast of hot water hits, and I slow it down to hours. The shock of the temperature and the pores opening. It's awesome. Relaxing. I hear a slow thump, like a concussive explosion. It's one of my roommates, knocking on the bathroom door. It can wait. The world can wait. My life can wait.

HORSEMEAT

BIG MIKE IS sitting on the hood of the truck when I get off work. He's eating grilled chicken breasts out of a sack, without joy, a bored consumption of meat. Bodybuilders burn five or six thousand calories a day, an amount that would afford most people cronuts and pints of ice cream, but they apathetically eat protein sources. It's fuel, not really food anymore.

Jesus, Mike, what are you doing here?

I need the truck again.

I can't keep taking it out. It's not a Zipcar.

A thousand bucks is your end, bro.

That's all I need to hear. A thousand dollars would solve all of my immediate financial problems at home and leave me a little to have fun with.

Big Mike hands me one of those old-school coke bullets.

Happy Birthday, he says.

It's not my birthday, I tell him, trying to work the bullet right.

No, that's the name of this shit. Do it. You'll thank me later.

I give it a snort. There's a blinding flash that almost knocks me over, an amphetamine kick, and then all I can smell is birthday cake. And there's a high, a very specific high: it's that rushing joy you get as your mom brings out the birthday cake.

Make a wish, he says.

I go back inside for the keys.

On the back wall of the slaughterhouse, there's a mural of a happy farm with cartoony pigs and cows all having a great time.

The cruel thing about it is, the barn door in the painting is the entrance to the killing floor. The animals, if they could think like we do, would think they're going to a better farm. Weird sense of humor, but if you work in a slaughterhouse, I guess you have to have one. Glad all I can smell is birthday cake. There's dead shit everywhere—must be horrible. I don't like being high in a place like this, but it's great to have the one sense knocked out.

The butcher who cut up our racehorse is a man who looks like a human version of a pug. He has deep wrinkles in his forehead and eyes that seem on the verge of popping out of their sockets. I think he's Russian, but I'm not sure. It's an accent similar to that, but he won't talk to me, only to Big Mike in hushed tones.

After the slaughterhouse, we end up at a warehouse in Oakland. It looks abandoned, dirty, broken windows along the side. A row of dilapidated RVs are parked outside.

We pull around to a loading dock with a roll-up door. Big Mike gets out and bangs on it with his fist. Squeaking and creaking, it rolls up.

Five feet of muscle stands behind the door. The guy looks like Mighty Mouse. I've never seen a guy this short with a chest this big. If he weren't wearing a cut-up shirt, I would think it was fake. Tiny legs, enormous chest, huge head. Behind him is a row of carts.

Mighty Mouse hops on the truck. He tosses the packages into the cart like they were the evening paper.

Mike walks past the roll-up door and motions for me to follow with an evil grin. I hear screams and horrible grunts that sound like a hippo vomiting. A smell follows. It's like spaghetti sauce heated in a microwave with a faint hint of chlorine.

I need another hit of Happy Birthday.

Mike hands it over. Snort, flash, and the smell of birthday cakes. Your friends may be unpredictable and flaky, but drugs will always be exactly what they are.

This is the real deal, bro, a real gym for real lifters. Mike slaps me on the chest when he says it.

The powerlifters are first. Walking around the gym, they don't look that impressive. Frankly, they look like a bunch of fat guys, but they're built for nothing but strength. How much weight can a man lift once? That's what they aim to find out. That's their reason for living.

There are rows of squat racks, bars bending on the backs of men built like refrigerators. Their asses come much closer to the ground than I could get mine without a bar, the kind of squat only toddlers and the third-world poor seem to pull off, like they're trying to shit in a hole in the ground.

Next are the deadlifters, some with what must be close to a thousand pounds, men with pumpkin heads that turn bright red as they lift the weights, accented by the chalk dust in the air. They're screaming like they're victims of some kind of Catholic inquisition.

Bench pressers, each with two spotters, lift and scream while the spotters yell what are supposed to be encouraging phrases but sound more like threats to me. Did you know there's such a thing as a bench-press shirt? There is. Big Mike told me about them once but they don't sound like they would help.

Beyond the powerlifters are the strongmen. They've gone from the circus sideshows to the shittier timeslots of ESPN's other channels. These guys are like the powerlifters but for weird shit.

There are Atlas stones, which are giant concrete balls that you're supposed to lift up onto a pedestal. They clean and jerk giant logs with handles. Two guys toss a masonry block back and forth.

Some guys flip tractor tires. Another couple of guys slam a tire with a sledgehammer. Guys lift bars with strands of chains attached beside the weights.

Then, there's a whole group of guys I don't know what they're training for. In one corner, a Russian growls and yells at a flight of kettlebell lifters. At the opposite end, guys in Speedos curl and press dumbbells in front of a mirror. Two guys alternate dips like a pair of pistons. There are pull-ups with weights chained to the waists. Medicine balls. Indian clubs. Battle ropes. Sandbags.

Past that, there's saunas, steam rooms, tanning beds, and a cold plunge. Russians hitting a guy with a branch. Masseuses that look more like old butchers pounding on living slabs of flesh, blank-faced old men twisting and stretching the bodies into pretzels as their victims scream in agony.

Then shit gets weird.

There's a giant Swede with a live goat on his shoulders on a stairclimber wearing nothing but a pair of tighty-whities. I see the goat shit on him, but he doesn't stop. The thing that freaks me out is that he looks bored.

A fat black man wearing a sumo thong does squats, and every time he stands up, a fat white guy wearing a sumo thong punches him in the stomach. I can only assume they're taking turns.

There's a skinny German walking around in a lab coat with a jet injector. Lifters flag him down, and he comes by and injects them, like the way they used to do mass vaccinations. I can only assume it's roids. But who knows with these freaks? There's probably some next-level shit they're doing.

Big Mike gives me the rundown. They're buying the horse-meat because the French bodybuilder Serge Nubret ate something like four pounds of it a day when he was training. In the offseason, he supplemented that with a pound of rice and a pound of beans.

Four pounds. That's a lot. Take the patties out of sixteen quarter pounders. There's a lot of guys who can eat one pound of meat. But four, every day? That's a whole different kind of thing. It's hundreds of grams of protein. The thing is, these guys need it just to maintain their bodyweight.

The horsemeat is tainted with all kinds of drugs. Unless the horse is a stud candidate, they burn those poor fuckers out until they drop dead. They're pumped with the same drugs you would give an athlete, but crazy horse-powered versions for enormous hearts and a few extra miles of circulatory systems. But this crowd is made of the last people who would give a fuck about having drugs in their meat. Hell, they probably pay extra for it.

In his office, Mighty Mouse cuts lines of a pale green powder I don't recognize on his desk.

What is this? I ask.

Doesn't have a name yet. It's good though. Painkiller. Takes out the soreness in the muscles without making you tired. Want a bump?

Always, I say.

I lean over and snort half a line in each nostril. Feels good right away. Counters a raw feeling I didn't notice I had. I can't handle the wear and tear like I used to. I'm a senior citizen in drug years.

You like danceclubs? he asks, thumbing and fingering his nose to get all the crumbs.

I like the drugs at danceclubs. If the drugs are good enough, I like the music, too.

Mighty Mouse takes us to Pumps. It's a gay club where the bodybuilders dance on platforms. I've never been here. Middle-aged men wait to get in, a few old geezers mixed in.

We skip the line, a hulking mass pulls the rope aside, and we walk in. The bass beats rattle my molars. Most of the clientele is slender gay men with a thing for huge men. Some like the cut bodybuilders; some want the biggest man possible. Some want them smooth and oiled; others want the hairy, pro-wrestler-looking guys. Big-screen TVs on the walls are showing *Conan the Barbarian*. We follow through the crowd up a flight of stairs and through a door, down a hallway, and through another door.

There's a whole bar upstairs no one's in but one bartender. There's no music up here, but we can still feel the vibrations of the bass beats. Life-size pictures of bodybuilders of days past adorn the walls: Arnold, Ferrigno, Dave Draper, Sergio Olivia, Serge Nubret, and even Eugen Sandow.

Mighty Mouse leads us to a table and motions for us to take a seat. He waves at the bartender. Three vodkas and a Tupperware container arrive. He opens the container and slides it toward us. It's a powder, looks like Tang.

Check it out, fellas, he says. *Our new proprietary club drug. Made exclusively for use at Pump. We call it Pump, of course.*

Proprietary drugs are the hot thing right now at clubs. You custom-order your own drug to match the mood of the club you run, and a Dutch chemist designs it for you and sends the formula to a lab in China, and then you get it discreetly shipped to you labeled as something else, like laundry detergent or some shit. You get a pallet of drugs—literally a ton of drugs dropped off for you at the docks.

Anyone can get the same music at clubs, but you can only get Freakout at Club Freakout, Boogiewoogie at Get Down, and Yeah Baby at Shagadelix. It's great for the club experience because everyone's on the same shit, and it's pretty much impossible to police as it's hard for a cop to prove that a new mysterious substance is actually an illicit drug unless he takes it and starts tripping balls.

So if you design the most popular drug, you have the most popular club. There's no better draw to a club, if you ask me. Drugs and clubs go hand in hand. People need somewhere to get high and people to get high with. They need the anonymity of the darkness and the music to keep them from having to talk to people. You can pump in whatever smell you want. You can change the lighting. People taste what you have in the club. So you're controlling every aspect of the experience, and if you control the drugs, you control the way all of those aspects are perceived.

Mighty Mouse spoons a small amount in the vodkas. You don't have to twist my arm. My favorite drugs are free drugs.

What's in it? I ask. Not that I care, really, just curious.

The usual dance-club mix: a little bit to keep you up, a little bit to make the music sound good, a little bit to make you want to touch the other homely fuckers in the club. But the thing that's going to make me a rich man is a thermogenic. It actually burns more calories than the vodka contains. You can drink all night and actually lose weight. Do you have any idea how popular this is going to be with gay men and women?

I take a drink. Tastes like grapefruit juice that went bad.

This is fucking horrible. I shake the taste out of my head. Then, like the problem addict I am, I finish it in a big shot.

And it makes you sweat a little more than normal. And if you drink too much, it probably will induce renal failure. And fuck up your endocrine system over the long haul. But hey, did I tell you you'll lose weight? You'll never go broke underestimating the vanity of the American public.

The pump comes on slowly. This song sounds great. I know I'm high when I like this fucking music. I know objectively it's horrible, but it's sounding good right now. I feel like I look better. Better? Hot. Yes, I look good. Hot enough to fuck. God damn, this shit is good.

Mighty Mouse takes us downstairs to see what he calls the Big Show. He won't tell us what that is. Right now, I don't care. I will fuck whatever it is.

On stage, a Hulk Hogan impersonator and an Andre the Giant impersonator are singing "You're The One That I Want" from the *Grease* soundtrack. They look pretty good, but they're not the same size as the originals. They're normal-sized people, and it looks weird. Fake Andre is only like, five eight, and his wig is coming off. I think this is the Big Show, but I'm wrong. It's the end of the show right before the Big Show. Fake Hulk and Fake Andre have a big finish, with Fake Andre jumping into Fake Hulk's arms. They pose for the adoring crowd, then scatter off stage, taking props with them.

There's a lag in the music and a drug-stoked tension in the air. Gay catcalls ring out. Everyone's clearly waiting for whatever's about to happen.

The DJ plays a mashup of *Godzilla* music, Bonnie Tyler's "Holding Out for a Hero," and "Big Bad John." Fuck, I am high. The crowd goes fucking nuts, and I go nuts, too. I'm cheering. For what, I don't know. But they're excited, and I'm one of them. We're excited. Holy shit, what the fuck is coming? I yell for it to come out, whatever or whoever it is.

Through the crowd, a man walks, and as he gets closer, I can see he's completely naked. He's oiled up, shining like a fish pulled out of the water. His face has all the expression of a mannequin.

I see everyone looking at him. We're all high on the same shit. We're a crowd of horny lizards. We want to consume; to eat, fuck, and kill. They're higher than I am, which puts them completely beyond humanity. And they look great. Great in the way tweakers and junkies look great right before they go to shit. It's the thermogenic in the drinks. They're burning calories faster than they can eat them, but who gives a fuck when you're thin, right? Their eyes are all the same. They're all looking at this man walking through the crowd, the champion of Pump.

He takes the stage, and you know, I haven't seen a whole lot of cocks, but I doubt I'll ever see another one this big. It's hanging there like a sock with a cue ball in it.

A bass beat kicks in, and a look of fierce determination takes over his face. It's like he's angry, but not at anyone. He grits his teeth and begins sweating in front of us, and I realize he's not oiled—he's slickened with his own sweat, and it runs off him in a slow sheet.

Slowly his cock awakens, like a cobra coming out of a snake charmer's basket. The crowd roars its approval. I cheer too, and although I know I could really give a shit, it's impressive seeing a cock this big get hard in front of everyone. He must be getting light-headed.

When it's fully hard, it looks around the room with its hideous gaping mouth-eye. His eyes are closed and his head is tilted back. I would think he's passed out, but he's still upright and his fists are clenched so hard his arms are shaking. The crowd can't take it. Men shove their way to the front. Bodybuilder bouncers keep them from rushing onto the stage.

The man stands there, his cock quivering, like it's having a nightmare or it's confused or something. It swells and pulsates. Veins throb on the shaft and on each fist, running up in gutters across his arms, up his neck, and into little squiggles on his forehead.

How long this goes on, I can't tell. I've lost track of time. He's glowing bright red as his capillaries swell and burst.

Precum glistens off the head of his cock, a simple milky tear, and now I know what the Big Show is. I back up through the crowd, trying to get as far away from the stage as possible. His penis shakes at us like an old man's angry fist, and then it happens.

A shot of cum like the ghost of a snake shoots out, and men jump to catch it like it's a free T-shirt at a stadium. It's followed by short angry jizz bursts. The man's yelling, but I can't hear him over the noise of the crowd. The spectators rush the stage and dog-pile him. I head out the door. I need some air, but nothing is going to top that. Maybe ever.

The cool night air of Folsom Street hits me. I'm soaked with sweat. I didn't notice so much inside, but out here, it's freezing.

A dank, sour, shit smell hits me. I look for a pile of bumarrhea but don't see anything. I must be coming down off the birthday cake.

A convertible Jaguar rolls by us. I want to fuck it. Those curvy, beckoning lines. The light changes, and the driver hits the gas, leaving brakelights trailing like toothpaste in its wake.

THE BOSS

MY ARM HURTS. It's wet. I look down. I'm at work. Arm's in a tank. Moby Dick whale biting the fuck out of me. Fucker. I hate this guy. He lives up to the dick part of his name. Dick. Asshole whale. I wrestle him a while. The only way to get him to let go of you is to stick a finger in his blowhole. I jam my finger in knuckle-deep, and he lets go and swims to the corner of his tank.

I don't remember coming in. This isn't good. Entire chunk of lost time. I remember the gym. Going to Pump. The Big Show. Being on the curb, sweating my ass off. Then I'm here. Hell. Something's wrong. I need to fix my mix. More drugs? Different drugs? Less mixing the drugs? More of just one?

Eirean rolls in, literally, on a pair of vintage Nike disco skates. He's wearing his best power-plaid flannel. There must be a meeting today.

Eirean O'Malley, the boy genetic genius. The guy who figured out the dwarf genome in the whales. The man who made an empire of making the world's biggest mammal into the world's most collectible.

Eirean is barely into his twenties. Drives a Tesla Roadster, owns a pair of Tibetan dogs he bought from a temple while on a trip and bribed them back to the US. He has a condo in one of those mirrored buildings that stands tall over the Bay Bridge on-ramp. He's a rich fucker selling things to other rich fuckers.

Chuck, bro, we need to talk.

Fuck, I think, I'm caught for something. I could be busted for any number of things.

What's up, boss?

I have a client coming in later. I need something special for the party.

Ah, hell. This is why I don't get fired. If you come into work drunk, you can get fired, but if you're a great drug connection, you'll never get fired. Your only worry is that some other degenerate fuck with a better phone full of contacts doesn't get hired.

What are you looking for? Psychedelics? Amphetamines? Designer stuff?

No. Something special. Something not on the market yet.

How am I supposed to get something that's not on the market?

I don't know, figure it out. Should I ask where you're going in the company trucks in the mornings? Should I ask why you sometimes stand in front of the tank and do nothing but stare for an hour? Should I ask why someone drank your Vitamin Water by accident from the fridge and didn't come down for two days?

That shit was clearly labeled as mine.

Not the point. I know what's going on with you. Frankly, I don't give a fuck. But you need to do this for me.

OSO

I CAN SMELL Oso from outside his building. He's up a few floors, but he leaves a trail of his funk behind. It's not bad out here, but it's rough up close. It's a sour smell, like something went bad. It's a quick-hitting smell, like when you open a container and sniff, and everything's fine until you're about to pass out. Some people say that it's a fat-guy smell, that he can't wash himself. But I think it's worse than that. I know someone who did time with him, said he would take a full shower and would come out still stinking, said a celly hanged himself because they wouldn't transfer him out, said he got shanked one time, and the fat closed over both the sharpened spoon and the guy's hand, and Oso beat him to death while he was stuck there like that, because he was that weird fat-guy strong, slow, but hit like a mule kick. I've walked into clubs and known he was in there because of the smell.

Oso is easily five hundred pounds. Maybe he's six. I don't know. I don't have a reference for anyone being that huge. Three hundred, I've seen, and he's well past that. When he sits, parts of him hang over other parts of him. When he stands, parts of him don't get up when other parts get up. He's not shaped like a human anymore.

He doesn't leave his Tenderloin apartment often, but when he does, everyone gets out of the way. He wears a black outfit and floats through the sidewalks. His street name is The Death Star, but no one says that to his face. He has his groceries and drugs delivered, so when he leaves the apartment, he's only leaving to kick some ass. No one knows who it will be, but they know to run.

Pity the poor fuck who doesn't see him coming. His rage matches his appetite. I've seen him pin a junkie against a car with his belly, like a fat fleshy airbag, in a suffocating gesture. Your body immediately exhales then can't inhale. There's no more panic than the lack of air.

What you fools looking for? Oso slurs.

He's eating a pie with a fork. Not a slice of pie, but a pie with a fork. He stops intermittently to spray more whipped cream into it.

Something special, I say. *Something not on the market yet. Something new.*

How much you fools looking to spend?

Not a dime over five large.

In his apartment with Big Mike, I'm the smallest man in the world. I'm trying to picture dropping three hundred pounds of fat on Big Mike, what would happen to his prison tats, but I can't formulate it in my head. Both of these guys started out at around nine pounds as babies and now they're enormous.

We cleared five grand in the horsemeat deal. Had to pay off the racetrack guy, and the gym was buying the meat wholesale. So we're trying to buy something from Oso.

I think I got the thing for you fools, he says with a snicker. He puts the pie down and reaches behind his chair, retrieving a lidded jar that's full of black marbles.

Bro, what is that? Big Mike asks.

Shit is too new for a name.

That's what we're looking for, I say. *What's it do?*

It's a synthetic smokeable speedball. Comes on speedy, then, where the crash would be, a nice Oxy-style comedown.

Great, I tell him. *How much for the jar?*

Fuck, you fools ain't buying the jar. These retail at a thousand bucks apiece.

No way, Big Mike says, standing up. *We're out. You're fucking with us.*

Wait, wait, I haven't told you the best part yet . . . this shit doesn't run out.

Now I'm interested, Big Mike says.

I've been hitting my own every day for a month; it's still the same size. I'll give you fools eight for five.

Too much, Big Mike says, *I don't know anyone who can afford it.*

I do, I blurt out. This is exactly what I need.

DRUGSITTER

NOT ONLY DO I have to find these rich fucks drugs, but apparently I have to babysit them as well—Eirean and four of his friends, with names like Colin and Taylor and Colby or whatever. They're all vaping; it smells like they're freebasing Jolly Ranchers.

Eirean's friends are exactly what I thought they would be: a bunch of nerds under thirty with more money than most suckers will ever see in a lifetime. What do they spend it on? New Balance jogging shoes, tight pants, plaid shirts, Tesla Roadsters, air hockey tables, and studio apartments that rent for as much as homes sell for in the Midwest. And occasionally, they spend a thousand bucks getting high.

We're on one of those bullshit bachelor-party-bus buses, the ones that look like a commuter shuttle got gutted and decorated like a casino, with LED lights everywhere and a stripper pole. It's the absolute opposite of cool.

Fuck it. I don't care. I sold five marbles, got our money back, and still have three left over. One for me and two more to sell. If I had a drug that wouldn't run out, I would definitely share it. But each of these rich fucks wants his own.

We're hitting this shit and watching *FernGully: The Last Rainforest* on DVD. The guys are pointing out how *Avatar* totally ripped it off. I've never seen this shit before. I was a full-grown man getting high and fucking women when this shit came out.

This whole hipster generation is stuck in their childhoods. I guess they had nice childhoods. They were told they were special and given lots of shit, they felt free to take out enormous student loans, and they do not give a fuck about what came before them. They had bike helmets and car seats and no one ever smacked them in the face for talking back.

They stop for cupcakes. I stay in the bus. I can't get out. I can't bear this bullshit. There's this huge line down the block, but they use a linecutter app and swap places with people near the front of the line for a fee.

They come back in the bus with bacon–German chocolate cupcakes. They take bites but don't finish them. They're too high to eat.

The marbles are much better than Oso let on. Whatever this shit is, it's clean. The world goes from standard definition to HDTV.

We stop at a club. Now it's on, I think, party time, but I'm wrong. As we're ushered into a private room, I'm still excited. But instead of strippers, it's videogames. Japanese shit that's not out here yet. They came to a club to get high and play videogames. For the love of fucking god.

GOOD MORNING

I WAKE UP with a sticky note on the floor next to my head. It says, *Who are you?* It looks like a girl's handwriting. I'm not sure whose floor this is. It's daytime. I check for my drugs, wallet, keys, and phone. All there. I'm wearing clothes and shoes. Time to go.

I go out the front door and enter a hallway. I'm either in a new apartment building or a really swank hotel. I find an elevator and get in.

In the reflection of the elevator wall, I see there's something spattered on my face. Little dots of something. I can't tell exactly what.

I check my phone's map. The pin drops at First and Harrison. Not bad. I know how to get home from here.

On First Street, a homeless man approaches me with a blind rap about needing food and a place to stay. It's eight AM. There are a lot of places to eat in San Francisco at this moment. Also, never bullshit a drug addict about drugs. We're all liars, and it takes one to know one. But when he gets close, his eyes widen, and he apologizes and runs. Whatever.

FRANK'S COFFEE

FRANK'S COFFEE IS the last of the '90s-style coffee-houses in San Francisco. It's a vestige of the past. All the new places are one-cup-at-a-time types. Frank's used to be a central meeting place of all of SF subculture. Now it serves the twenty or thirty badly aging hipsters left from then.

Faded tribal tats with fallout done at Erno's by Greg Kulz. Ripped-open flesh tats with biomechanics underneath. White-boy dreadlocks turned whiteman dreadlocks recede on skulls. Nose rings older than the average barista hang from septums. Old men who used to be young men who dressed like old men are now unironically dressed like old men. Giant cell phones sit on tables. People are reading books instead of Kindles. Bukowski. Bulgakov. Henry Miller. Hubert Selby. The same bullshit they tried to impress people with all those years ago.

Trashy paperbacks fill the shelves. Framed Frank Kozik posters from the Kilowatt and the Kennel Club decorate the walls. A big *NO CELL PHONES AT THE COUNTER* sign hangs below the cash register. Some kind of leafy plant that is somehow still alive hangs from the ceiling like it always has. Twenty-five-year-old staples from flyers are still in the wall. Jane's Addiction, *Ritual de lo Habitual*, on a cassette taped off a CD, hangs in the air like a bad smell.

More consistent than anything else is the manager, Joel. Joel's first job in San Francisco was bussing tables and cleaning up here while he was living at the hostel that used to be across the street, which, of course, is now a condo complex. Hundreds of employees have come and gone, but he's still here.

Joel pours me an iced coffee when he sees me walk in. He knows what I like. I've ordered more than a thousand of these from him, never changed the order.

I give him three bucks.

You have blood on your face, he says in a monotone.

What?

It's not a lot. But you should clean it off. It's creepy.

I'm not sure what it is . . .

I am, he says, handing me the keys to the bathroom. *I'll watch your coffee.*

Freshly cleaned face and a coffee later, I'm strolling back through the Mission. There's something heavy in my pocket. I pat it down. The marble. I could use a hit. No pipe.

I know a store that sells squares of tinfoil. They also sell Brillo chunks and glass stems. At night, they sell Styrofoam cups of Royal Gate Vodka for a dollar to the local drunks.

When I get to the corner where it is, I'm looking at a fucking baby store that specializes in its own locally sourced organic baby food. For the love of fuck. I'll have to wait till I get home.

At home. In my room with the door shut. Noise-cancelling headphones. Black Sabbath's *Master of Reality.* Fill the pipe, hit the marble. Eyes closed. Perfect. I dig around for my remote. Shit, it's almost out. But I'll worry about getting more later. I drop a little in the eye, speed up the iPod, and listen to what sounds like normal speed to me.

Life is good when the drugs are good.

●

I wake up. I feel refreshed. This may be normal for some people, but not for me. I usually wake up needing something or recovering from something, but never feeling better than I did the day before. I feel . . . healthy. Which isn't right. Maybe I woke up still high? Am I high or not?

I take a hit of the coffee. It's rancid. Gone bad. I pop the top, and there's moldy skin underneath. How long was I out? I thought I just took a nap. I was dead to the world, long enough for a layer of scum to form across the top of the coffee.

What day is it? That's how you know the drugs are good. When you honestly don't know what day it is.

NSA ANDY

THE UNMISTAKABLE SMELL of human shit hits me as I turn the corner on Valencia Street. It smells like shit that went bad, if that's possible. It's as if it's filling the street; I can't imagine the source. It's like when you're in a bathroom and someone has shit on the floor, or taken such a long shit that the top of it sticks out of the water like the Loch Ness Monster. That smell.

I could be high in the way that this would ruin my day. But I'm high in the other way, where I can deal with it. What I see, though, is too weird even to come from a drugged-out mind. This is so fucked up, it's a lucid bit of reality. Sometimes you're too high to deal with anything, and sometimes you're high enough that you can deal with anything at all.

There's a shitman trying to get into a vintage furniture store.

When I say shitman, I mean he's covered in shit; he's not smeared with it, but it's piled and clumped on him. To the point where I can't tell if he's wearing clothes or not, but I'm guessing not. It's like the Human Torch but with shit instead of fire. He looks like a six-foot-tall limbed turd with two eyes and a mouth.

There's a young hipster employee fending him off with a child's prayer bench, like a lion tamer's stool. Shitman's yelling crazy shit, wearing crazy shit, clearly shit-crazy. Apeshit. Batshit. Humanshit.

But of course I know this fucker. Somehow through all the brownness, I recognize him as a guy we call NSA Andy.

NSA Andy, story goes, used to be a codebreaker for the NSA. Damn good one, some kind of math savant, the type they recruit. There's a flagged question in the SAT test, one you can only truly solve if you are in an elite class of mathematicians. Of course, people will get it by accident, but if you get it right, the NSA tracks you and evaluates your skills covertly. They watch your passwords, your PIN numbers, that kind of thing. If you have potential, they approach you.

So NSA Andy gets flagged and followed. They pick him up in the place where they find the kind of mathematicians they want: rehab. There are those who are good at math, but the ones who will create the next-level shit are damaged goods. They're insane or drug addicts or both. They're also the ones whose lives have fallen apart. They pick the math freaks who need a way out of whatever shit they're in.

For a while, NSA Andy lives the life. They set him up with an apartment that completely caters to his needs. They bring him food, coffee, drugs, cigarettes, and anything else he wants. All he has to do is solve an equation that is slipped under his door every morning.

There's a whole dorm full of these guys, each one working on small bits of one really huge math problem, none of them knowing what the others have. But good old Andy, he didn't sleep like everyone else. He had time to kill. The equations were delivered at five AM every morning. After they were distributed, he sneaked up and down the hallways, sliding out equations from underneath the doors, memorizing them, and re-sliding them back under the doors.

NSA Andy saw something while he was there, like a code or an algorithm for everything: government passwords, Vatican secrets, missile launch codes, muffin recipes, the secret formula for Coke, horse-racing trifectas, next year's Super Bowl score, and the locations of the planet's uranium. It's all some complex code he developed and turned in.

Once the government had it, they needed to eliminate it from him. They put noise-cancelling headphones on him and played an MP3 of a series of words that erased the part of his brain that contained the code and replaced it with the lyrics to every sitcom theme known to man. Then, done with him, they released him back to the wild.

At least that's how he tells it.

Now he works endlessly to recreate the code; you see him scribbling away on the backs of flyers, with Sharpies on the blank sides of box trucks, with chalk on the sidewalk. All the while, he sings theme songs, trying to find the numbers once again, get things to line up right.

He's singing the theme to *The Courtship of Eddie's Father* with anger, purpose, and a dark helplessness.

The shit is new. Haven't seen him covered in shit before.

I get closer. A cop car and an ambulance pull up.

You can't get away with this on Valencia Street. Maybe in '89 or something, but the day a naked man can cover himself in shit and do his own thing in the Mission is over. What's happened to this neighborhood? Even Capp Street is respectable now.

I see that there's a layer of old, flaky, dry shit dusting in the air. But on top is an application of fresh, wet, glistening shit. He's been at this for a while.

The cops and the EMTs are arguing. Who takes this? Who wants a shit-covered man singing about his best friend at the top of his lungs? The hipster yells, *SOMEONE FUCKING TAKE HIM.* The prayer bench is getting heavy, I guess.

Some time goes by, and animal control shows up. This guy is

pissed as well. *Not an animal,* he says. *Fuck this.* The cop orders him to get him. *I don't take orders from you,* he says.

Now it's a four-way fight of who wants him least. Across the street, the smell hits a woman, who vomits her Tartine pastries on her Lexus crossover. That's going to fuck up the paint job. There are camera phones out; it's all going down on video.

The animal-control guy snags Andy's right arm with this loopy-pole thing they use to wrangle angry dogs. The Vietnamese guy from the liquor store comes out with a hose with a pistol-grip sprayer and removes the shit in a power blast, like Rambo in the basement of the police station, all the while smoking a Marlboro Red without touching it, the smoke around his head like Einstein's hair. And did I call it right or what? Andy is god damned naked. Still singing. That man never gives up.

BACK TO WORK

COPS ARE ALL around MiniWhale when I show up. Ambulance. Fire Marshal. It's a city-paid party over here. What the fuck is going on? They're taping off the scene. Something big has happened. I thought I was done with the law-enforcement part of my day.

Sir, step back, a cop says.

Sir? He looks like a kid. Cops keep getting younger, but I stay the same age. I see the young ones like this, want to ask if their moms know they're out this late. I want to tell them, *It's dangerous out here, young man, why don't you go on home?* But you can't talk to cops that way. I put on my most adult authoritarian face.

I work here. What's going on?

As the words come out of my mouth, I know I'm still high. Nothing like talking to a cop to set you straight on that. Pulse rises. Fuck, can he tell? Do I look high?

He calls the detectives over. They want to know all sorts of shit. Do I work there, what's my position, how long have I worked there, did I work with Eirean O'Malley. Why are they using the past tense?

What's going on? I say, in my best indignant tone.

Sweat. A thin layer bursts and covers me like a malfunctioning force field.

They keep with their questions. It's making the drugs kick in harder. They sound like *Despicable Me* minions.

WHAT'S HAPPENING, GOD DAMN IT, I DEMAND TO KNOW.

Sir, you'll have to calm down a bit. We have some really serious news for you.

So they found Eirean in some kind of nasty dead state: gutted, ribs spread open, missing all the organs. Hollowed out on top of the air hockey table. No signs of forced entry. Inside job, or someone he knew.

I remember the blood on my face. Could I have been there for that? Was I that high that I don't remember eviscerating Eirean? Or did I witness it? Or did I get away?

Whichever way, if I was involved, the guy who did this or the cops will be after me soon enough. I need to bust out of here.

I should cry or freak out or something. But I'm still way to wrecked on this marble stuff to give a good god damn. They're talking and asking questions.

Sorry, I say. *State of shock. Can we talk later?*

The detective hands me a card.

The whales. It hits me; no one's been taking care of the whales. And then it hits me as well that no one will notice if the whales are missing.

Fuck, the whales.

Fuck the whales? he asks.

No, oh fuck, what ABOUT the whales? . . . I need to get in there. I need to take care of those little guys, or they're all going to die. Today's the day we're supposed to transport all the whales to the other facility. It's okay; I won't need the rec room.

He waves someone else over to escort me in. I get to where the whales are and turn on the powered pallet jack.

You know how to use one of these? I ask.

Yeah, used to work at Costco.

San Francisco's finest. Protecting our streets because it pays better than ten-pound jars of mayonnaise.

Together we load the whales. All twelve whales here. One point two million dollars worth of whales. They're going on the big truck. And I'm taking this truck and never coming back. Fuck the whales? Nah. Sell the whales.

Hey buddy, wanna buy a whale? Shhh. Not so loud . . .

Junior Blue gets a buzz on his phone. It's a text. He pulls it up. A link. *Holy shit*, he says, and he laughs. *Look at this*, he says, shoving the phone in my face.

It's Shitman-Andy. Shitmandy? The clip is already up on YouTube. It's going viral.

FUCK IT ALL

I HAVE TO clear my shit out and get my stash and whatever cash I have. I'm not coming back. Burn the roomies for the bills, fuck 'em. They can sue me, come after me, call a cop—they're already looking for me. Fuck this.

Fuck this apartment, this flat, all the San Francisco rooms for rent—they're too small, they're not heated, there's mold everywhere. Six people to five bedrooms, sometimes more. No living rooms. Water heaters for two service three times that many. Thin walls, hollow-core doors, upstairs tap dancing neighbors. Tinderbox buildings one knocked-over candle away from a bonfire.

Fuck rent control. Fuck the guy who holds an eight-hundred-dollar lease and charges eight hundred bucks for each of the three rooms but calls himself an activist and an artist when he's not creative and lives a sedentary life. Fuck the old hippies with the great places they'll never leave.

Fuck the artists, the bands, and the poets for making this neighborhood cool and trendy and hip, for having poetry slams and DJ nights and galleries that showcase graffiti artists. First they come and give everyone else an excuse to show up, and before you know it, the rich fucks are moving in.

Fuck rich fucks driving up prices. If you refused to pay too much, the prices wouldn't rise like this. It's all your fault in the end. Fuck you and your desire to live in a neighborhood that won't make up for your lack of imagination or personality. Live somewhere else. If all of you move anywhere, the yoga studios and artisanal cheeseries will follow. I promise. You won't want for a thing. Ever.

Fuck California with its liberal reputation and conservative governors. Nixon, Reagan, Schwarzenegger. Pete Wilson, who cut the CSU budget year after year and built more prisons with the money. Why does California get a rep for being full of hippies? It's full of prisons and crumbling schools.

I look around the room. What do I need to take with me? Nothing. None of this. I don't need it. It's all garbage. Flyers, posters, books I'm not going to read, thrift-store clothes, and garage-sale records. VHS tapes and a VCR. A tube TV that weighs as much as I do. Bookshelves I found on the street. One fifteen-pound dumbbell that I've tripped over more times than I've lifted. What was I thinking with that?

I stuff underwear, socks, and a few shirts in a garbage bag. I have the shoes on my feet, and I've been wearing these jeans for weeks straight anyway. When I get where I'm going, I'll get new shit.

I should've bailed months ago. Years ago. I never should have come here. I should have left the country right after high school. Fuck it. Fuck it all.

DAVE KITCHELL

DAVE KITCHELL'S HANDS feel like bricks. They're cold, menacing, cable-fingered mitts. He has sharp calluses that pinch your hands when you shake his. But it's the inhuman hardness that really freaks me out. There's no fleshly give in his hands; they're too solid for that. If he held up his closed fists, it would look like he's holding an invisible bat.

Dave's a fearsome hitter. He bats fifth for the Giants. His average is low, but when he does make contact, it rarely stays in the park. He's adored by children, loved by the ladies, feared by opposing pitchers, and hated by the media. He's played longer than any current big leaguer, and his secret is that Big Mike has been selling him drugs for years.

Dave's body is a housing for a chemistry set. He's been on everything. Not just the ones you would assume, like steroids and amphetamines, but vanity drugs that work better than plastic surgery, and he chews mood stabilizers like they were Lucky Charms. He has an affinity for psychedelics and a particular appetite for military-combat drugs. I don't know how he cheats the league's drug testing, but he must be testing positive for everything.

Dave is notorious for bare-hand catching a bases-loaded line drive at third base. It broke one of his fingers, but he still stepped on third and threw to second for a triple play. His secret? He was geeked out of his mind on a number of drugs. He told me later that he didn't see the ball until it was right in front of his face, but it was floating in slow motion like a fist-sized piece of popcorn.

Dave's made over a hundred million dollars in salaries over the years, and, unlike many of his peers, he's made even more than that in his investments, both legal and otherwise. Laundromats, car washes, dog groomers, landscapers, tattoo shops, janitorial services, and apartment buildings cover the income from drugs, illegal furs and hides, and exotic animal importing.

You'll read stories about a boxer who owns a lion or a pop star who has his own giraffes. You can't just go down to the pet store and pick one up. You can't score a walrus in the park like a bag of weed. Sure, you can find a boa constrictor or maybe a ferret, but if your girlfriend wants a baby jaguar for her birthday, you're going to need someone with connections.

Now, a lot of people will ask why a guy who's made hundreds of millions still wants to live a life of crime. Well, the answer is, you don't get it. If you have to ask, you're not the kid of person who would understand or even accept the answer.

The man was a criminal before he was a pro ballplayer, and that's what he'll be when his body and the finest chemical science fail him. The baseball salary is only a nice cover for a massive financial empire.

Then there are the assholes who will ask what you could possibly spend that much money on. Whatever the fuck you want. What have you ever wanted? Do you want Beyoncé to sing at your birthday party? Do you want to sit in Spike Lee's seat at the Knicks game? Do you want to fuck the girls from *The Facts of Life*? Everything has a price. You may not get it, but if you have the money, people are open to negotiation.

But my dealing, of course, is with a truckload of whales. I have a truckload of dwarfed, cloned whales, and I need to move them fast, for cash, to someone who has the ability to sell off a dozen whales and doesn't care if they're legal or not.

●

Dave lives in a huge house in Fremont. Fremont's not what you think of when you think of multimillionaires or mansions. Most people in the Bay Area only know Fremont as a last stop on a particular BART line. Few people have been there who don't already live there.

We're met at the door by a man who I think used to be a lineman for the Raiders. His face looks like it's been hit by a shovel and healed over on a regular basis. There are thick, deep, faded scars across his eyebrows and his nose. He takes us down to the gym, where Dave is lifting.

Dave's gym looks like any chain gym, but he's the only one here. Cardio machines, free weights, the whole deal.

So, little man, what you thinking on price for these whales?

Got a dozen whales at a hundred K per. So I'm thinking six hundred wholesale.

If they was legit, maybe. I was thinking a hundred for the lot.

No fucking way.

You want to unload these fast?

I could sell one for that.

If they was legit, maybe.

These may be the last ones, ever. I'll go four hundred.

I have three hundred thousand in cash, here. You can walk out of here with it right now. It's half of what you were thinking, I know, but time is of the essence. And that's plenty to get you to wherever you're going. Truck included.

Deal, I say.

He sends a text. The Raider-butler arrives with three briefcases.

This is more money than I've ever seen in my life.

Dave gets a text. He looks at it and laughs. He holds it out to me. It's the video of Andy.

Look at this. Crazy motherfucker covered in shit.

WHERE TO GO

THE MAIN PROBLEM with this much ill-gotten funds is where to put it. Where can you stash it that other people won't take it? I can't travel the world with three suitcases full of cash. I can't clear customs with it. I can't throw it in the luggage rack of a greyhound. Right?

How do you sleep with the fear of someone taking a stash off you that big? I can't carry that around like Gollum's ring. It will be the end of me. It will make me crazy.

I have to invest it. But I can't leave a trail, either. So I have to invest it in something like a pot farm. Something else illegal that will pay off in the long run. Something that will give me an allowance and let me live the underground life to which I've become so accustomed.

But for now, I have money to spend and drugs to do. Life is good when you have money and drugs.

I buy a van from some jackass on Craigslist. Says it's his old band van. It's covered in stickers and has seen some miles. But it's big and it's American and it will blend in well enough in any city. There's a loft bed in the back with the idea that gear can go down underneath it, which is also the perfect hiding place for the cash. And there's no way that this guy can be sober long enough to report me if my face pops up anywhere.

I am now a man who lives in a van. I've come to that point in my life when living in a vehicle sounds like a good option. This is fucked up. But it's the best way to go right now until the heat dies down.

The back of a van is a womb. The belly of the whale. All that. It's a sanctuary from everything. The world. Cops. Success. Ambition.

Maybe I'll just drive until the money runs out. From here to there, one rest stop to another Walmart parking lot, little towns across America where they still look up to a guy who just says fuck it, I'll drive around in a van forever.

My only hesitation is the sex. I don't want to be stuck having sex only with women who will fuck guys who live in vans. That's a whole different world. I've lived in some real shitholes, but at least they had addresses and mailboxes. And hell. Somewhere to piss. A lady would have to make quite a few concessions to spend a night in the Dodge with me.

It's small, but it's home. And they'll never find me here.

I come out of a blackout as coke is coming up my nose. I'm in a bathroom of somewhere. Not sure where I am; it's a bar or club or something. Not sure. Looks familiar, but that doesn't mean anything.

I come out of the stall. I know this place. It's the Dog House, an all-night dance party south of Market. It also caters to a dom-sub clientele that's about being super nice and loving to your "dogs." It's not the humiliation kind of thing with the slave set. It's kinder and gentler, but it keeps the collars and the leashes and the chains. But some owners just love to spoil their dogs.

I'm wearing a VIP wristband, so there's no way I'm hanging out with the pedestrians on the floor. There's a mashup playing of "Blue Monday" and "Regulate." I get through the crowd of eyes and teeth glowing in the black lights, the Day-Glo hair, and the textural bliss of a mass of people. I must be really high. Forcing my way through the crowd feels like fucking.

The VIP area is full of owners at tables chatting with their dogs sitting on the floor. The dogs aren't wearing much: briefs only in the case of the boy dogs, which most of them are, and briefs and halter tops for the girl dogs. They don't talk, but they look dumbly happy at me as I walk by. I find an empty table and sit.

I check my phone. Messages and texts from the roommate, many more from former coworkers and MiniWhale clients. A detective handling the murder case. The texts are coming in as I look at them. There are hundreds of them. Shit is blowing up.

A lady owner approaches with a pair of little people dogs. She asks to sit. She says something. I just nod my head, but I can't hear.

CHUCK? she yells. *DO YOU REMEMBER ME?*

It's Liza, a dancer I had a thing for when I first moved here. We had sex once. I had wanted it since I first saw her, and then it was like nothing when it happened. Didn't feel like a fucking thing. I was embarrassed. I thought I sucked in bed or something, a lousy lay. A few weeks went by. Found out through her friends that she really liked me and was mad that I never called her back. I had no idea why she would like me. But I blew it, and I think about it all the time.

LIZA.

YES. ARE YOU INTO THIS SCENE? YOU DON'T HAVE A DOG.

HONESTLY I DON'T KNOW HOW I GOT HERE. WHAT ABOUT YOU?

THESE AREN'T MINE. I'M A DOGSITTER FOR THIS OLD GAY COUPLE.

I WONDERED.

DO YOU HAVE ANYTHING?

MOST LIKELY.

I search my pockets. About time for an inventory. In my jacket, there's a Pomade tin. I open it. It's full of coke.

JESUS CHRIST, CHUCK.

She takes it, taps a little out, and cuts it into lines. I look around. I don't know who's watching. She rolls up a bill.

CALM DOWN. YOU LOOK TOTALLY PARANOID.

You're not paranoid if they're really after you.

She snorts half a line with one nostril, then switches nostrils and inhales the other. She hands me the bill. I should say no, but I don't. I can't feel my face. I took some kind of painkiller before this, from the feeling of things.

Halfway up my nose, I feel my heart punching my ribcage. Fuck. Too much. I do the other nostril. I have to keep things even. I need to come down though. I look up. Liza's playing with my marble.

DON'T FUCK WITH THAT.

WHAT IS IT? A GOOD LUCK CHARM?

CAN WE GET OUT OF HERE?

She pauses. Her face goes blank, then confused, then happy.

YES.

I follow her through a succession of strobe lights, black lights, and fog. I can't feel my feet. I see all these women dressed in '70s punk makeup, Siouxsies and such—must be some kind of retro thing coming back. I like it. None of them make eye contact with me. Just like the punk girls I remember.

As soon as we make it outside, I'm cold and my ears are

ringing. There's a mist falling, a foggy damp towel freezing my bones. It shocks me with momentary sobriety. I feel a pull.

This way, she says.

The little pups pull her in their harnesses toward the car. They're in a hurry. No wonder, they're almost naked.

It's so weird running into you, she says, checking her phone as we scurry down the sidewalk.

Oh my god, she says. *So gross.*

She hands me her phone. It's the Andy video. I hand it back to her.

Saw it already.

We get to an SUV. She opens the door and whistles. The dogs scramble in.

How did you get here? she asks.

I don't know, I say.

She laughs. *You are a funny guy.*

We're at some queer house in Twin Peaks. Old-school SF homo. Not any of this new-money, high-tech bullshit. This belongs to some daddy from way back. Probably bought this for a hundred K back in the early '80s.

The place is immaculate but outdated. Still, it's a welcome sight compared with the IKEA nightmares going on now. Tom of Finland prints hang in the living room. There's a trophy case in the corner from some kind of Castro contest, and there's a leather hat hanging on the one of the trophies. Pictures of men in chaps and whisk-broom mustaches. There's a big-screen TV, but it's old, one of those things that weighs a god damn ton, with a VCR and tapes of all the old classics like *Auntie Mame* and *The Rose.*

The dogs immediately run for the sofa. Liza yells at them, and they scamper away.

Do you have to walk them, too?

They shit in the toilet, if that's what you're asking.

Yeah, that's what I'm asking.

Liza puts on a record. It takes a minute. It's *Jesus Christ Superstar* or *Hair* or some other '70s musical soundtrack.

I take out the marble and my pipe.

Now, for this . . . I say.

She turns off the lights and turns on a lava lamp. She joins me on the couch.

What is it? she asks.

Something new. The new thing. The new high.

She takes it without another word of what it does, what it's like, what's in it. It's the new high. The first time you get high on anything, it's full of promise, potential, probable bliss. Maybe it's going to be your favorite. Maybe it's the best yet. Maybe it's the drug that finally fixes you. But whatever it is, that first time is special. It's the one that feels the best. It's the time that you use to judge all following usages of that drug. She hits it, long and practiced.

In the light, I see some kind of textural problem with her face, like horrible acne or something covered by makeup. It's a bad scar, a huge one, running from her chin up to her hairline. I notice her ear; it's a prosthetic. It's hanging on, slightly off-colored. Her eye is dull, because it's not real, it's glass. Something horrible happened to a side of her face.

Jesus Christ, Chuck. This is good.

She holds it in with the patience of an Olympic diver. She exhales.

Oh my god. Oh my god. This is good. Fuck. This is good. Take your clothes off.

Really?

Yes, really, take them off, now. Oh god, I have to fuck on this.

She passes me the marble back. Immediately, her clothes come off, sliding out of them like a snake molting.

Her body is a mural of every trendy tattoo from the last twenty-five years. Some faded, some added to, some with fallout, some fresh. Tribal. Biomech. Traditional. Pinup. Roses. Fucking angel wings on her back.

There are stretch marks and scars, but it doesn't matter one bit. She still has those wide hips curving out from the narrow waist. I hit the marble and get marble-hard right away.

Come on, she says. *Off.*

She's rooting around for something. I'm trying to get my clothes off so quickly that I'm taking off my pants without taking off my shoes first. They're all tangled up and stuck. My cock looks like it's reaching for her.

She turns around with a bottle of lube the size of a Pringles can. She laughs.

Oh my god. Now that's the cock I remember so fondly. Let me.

She pulls my pants and shoes off. I'm naked on the floor. She opens the lube and pours it on me like she's syruping a pancake.

She sits down, and I'm inside her right away. I know I'm high, but I swear I'm hitting her fucking brain with my cock.

Oh my god, Chuck. Jesus Christ.

We fuck and we fuck and we fuck.

We hit the marble.

We fuck some more. It feels like I'm reaching weird places

inside her with my cock, like she's full of hollow tunnels and my cock is an eel.

Can I get some of that coke?

Yes, of course . . .

She reaches over without getting off me. Her ear falls off. I think I'm tripping. I'm not. She picks it up and puts it on the couch.

Ah, fuck, she says, *sorry. Lost the ear like ten years ago.*

I don't care . . .

She grabs the coke tin out of my jacket pocket and opens it. With her pinky fingernail, she scoops a blast up and snorts it. She hands me a fingernail full, and I take it straight up the nose.

It feels like an hour. There's remote in my system. I almost forgot about it. I haven't had withdrawals. The marble high counteracts it or something.

We fuck some more. Her hair slides to the side.

You don't mind, do you? It's a wig.

Help yourself . . .

She rips off her wig and throws it on top of her ear. There's bald scarring all over that one side of her head. Like a bad burn or acid scar or something, I don't know. Fuck it. Who cares. Somehow, it just makes her hotter.

HUNT'S

I'M DREAMING OF Twentieth and Mission. It's a completely lucid dream. More so than I've ever experienced. I know I'm dreaming because I'm outside Hunt's. It's the middle of the night, the best time to go. Hunt's was open all night. So many times after the bars and clubs closed, I ended up here. It was the only place in the Mission that was still open. Hunt's closed ages ago. It was my favorite donut place. Ever.

I walk in for a dream donut. I'm going to be a total pig before I wake up.

Buttermilk bar, with chocolate. Cruller. Apple fritter. Fuck it. One of each of each one that you have. Even the maple ones I don't like. One of each. Get a fucking box.

Why do all the donut places have pink boxes? Never any other color.

They're putting the donuts in the box when something disturbing walks by the window: me. It's me, the way I looked in 1990.

Just give me the box. Now. Here's twenty bucks . . .

There's no way I'm leaving the donuts here. Dream or not.

I run out of Hunt's. I follow behind 1990 me.

Hey, kid . . .

Can't help you.

No, it's not like that . . .

Fuck off, short eyes.

There's so many things to tell you about . . .

1990 me turns around, grabs my shoulders, pulls back, then gives a forward shove. I trip backward, dropping the donut box. Fuck. This hurts. 1990 me storms off, making tracks off to Seventeenth and Capp, where I lived back then.

I gather up my stuff. Shoving stuff back into pockets. Cruller on the street. Leave it. A crackhead in a hurry swoops it up like an owl snatching a mouse. If the crack hasn't killed him yet, a sidewalk pastry won't phase his system. Keys, get keys . . . no phone. Well, if it's 1990, I shouldn't have one.

Then I spot the marble on a dirt patch some damned tree is trying to grow out of. Did I have it with me? Is that my drug marble or a marble marble? Fuck it, take it.

So I need to know. Drug marble or no? Fuck it. Light it and find out.

In 1990 Mission, it's not hard to find a pipe. Walk down the street. Head shops where yoga studios will be. Mexican-farmer bar where the dyke bar shows up later. Used-furniture store will become the old-timey barbershop. The barbershop that becomes a crafts boutique.

Pipe. Torch lighter. Unlit doorway. Hiss of the flame in the night air. I'm smoking a fucking marble marble, a dirty, dirt-covered marble, a mocking little dumbass glass sphere.

Yo, son, what about a taste?

A silhouette leans in. Something hitting me in the gut. No breath. No air. Wind knocked out? Dying? Fuck. Pockets . . . hands . . . tugging. The donuts scattered on Capp Street, stepped on, soaking in drunks' piss. A jelly hemorrhages. Timberland comes closer to the face. The whole scene is a shrinking tunnel, getting smaller, until it's completely black.

I'm hitting the marble. Liza sits across from me. No wig, no ear. Smeared makeup like signal smoke. Orange-peel burn scars.

You okay? She says with a smirk and a giggle. *Don't forget to breathe.*

Yeah . . . fuck, had a really intense moment there. I thought I was dreaming. It was like I was back in 1990.

Trippy. How many hits do you get off this thing?

Don't know. Story is, never runs out.

Bullshit. What is it then?

I don't know, some kind of experimental drug . . .

It's not a drug.

Why?

Drugs run out. It's what they do.

You have a point.

Take coke. It's this thing that makes your life okay, no matter who you are, but the only catch is when this little pile of powder runs out, everything's fucked. You're living in an hourglass, and this magic sand is draining out this hole in your face. Worse. Your friend's face. Fuck your friend. She's the reason the pile is getting smaller and your life won't be okay anymore.

Yes, I see . . .

BUT YOU KNOW, FUCK EVERYONE, BECAUSE YOU CAN JUST GET MORE.

Hey, Liza . . .

I'm sorry. God. Look, if you take away the drugs that run out, then you take away getting more, and getting the money for more. And that's a drug addict's life. You can't just make a drug they don't have to get the money for or have to look for even when they have the money. That's part of the whole deal.

I don't think . . .

No you don't. Obviously. Do you think I would have worked at the Market Street Cinema all those years if I didn't need the money?

Of course not.

Well it's not that simple, asshole. I wanted to do that shit to myself, to lapdance guys who look like my dad, to blow them in the back for a tip, to catch weird shit all the time from wherever the fuck in the world they came from. I wanted to let Japanese perverts on business trips shit on me. Literally. The drugs? They were a good fucking excuse. Because if I had been doing that for any other reason, you would've said I had a problem. That something was wrong with me. But you and every other junkie with a cock still wants to fuck me because I'm something you can save or some shit, save me with your magic cock.

It's not like that . . .

Oh, now you want to mansplain to me what shit is like? Fuck you, Chuck. You act like some nice sensitive guy, but you're a horrible piece of man shit like the others. Fuck 'em and leave 'em. Fuck 'em and fuck 'em.

I should go . . .

First good idea you've had all damn day.

I get my shit. It's like a scavenger hunt. Boxer briefs pants socks shirt jacket wallet keys phone stash.

Leave me a bump.

Fuck, really?

Yes.

I dump out a little coke for her right on the table.

That good?

Yes. Can you get me one of those marbles?

Ha. I knew it.

Shut up. Can you get me one or not?

A thousand bucks.

Jesus, Chuck.

That's how much it is.
Ugh. okay. Fine. Get it. Call me when you get it.
Will do.
I leave.
Chuck? she says.
WHAT.
It's nice to have you back around.
Yeah. Just like old times.

Jill's bar across from the hospital is a good place to drink in the morning. After the midnight-to-eight shift, all the nurses from the ER come over and tell stories, one-upping each other with who saw the worst shit.

Hot nurses are an old joke of porn no one tells anymore. Are there still nurse porns being made? There's the weird latex rubber outfits on Halloween. That's about as close as it comes. But there are no hot nurses in the ER at General. But fuck it, they're fun to drink with.

There are black girls from Richmond, Filipinos from Daly City, a token white girl, but she acts like a *cholita*, outlined-lip makeup and everything.

Man came in saying he couldn't go number two. That's what he called it. Number two. Can you imagine? A grown-ass man saying "number two"? Well we give him the spiel. Laxatives, you know. The whole bit. Then we check for blockage. Sure nuff. You know what was up there? Barbie heads. That sick faggot stuck a whole load of Barbie heads up his ass and tried to deny it. But when they started coming out of there, he started to cry and confessed every-thing. Sick faggot fucked himself with a fucking Barbie doll and the head broke off and he came like a rope. Well then he had to get

more Barbies. Had to get off more. Thought he was pooping the
heads later . . .

ESPN is showing the previous day's highlights. Dave Kitchell
stands in the batter's box and takes a fastball on his arm. Doesn't
move. Doesn't flinch. *That's Dave being Dave*, the announcer says.
No, it's Dave geeked out of his mind. Followed by highlights of
the weirdest moments of his career. Breaking the bat over his leg.
The clubhouse tantrums. Charging Bob Saget during a celebrity
softball game for MTV. And finally, the barehanded catch.

I need to get out of town. But I don't feel like it right now.
There's too many things to do. I need drugs. I need a gun. Fuck.
I need a gun. I need to keep someone from taking this shit.
And I'm not being taken alive. Fuck that. A guy like me can't
function in prison. I know guys who would love an excuse to
do nothing but read, jerk off, and work out. Not me. I need my
freedom. And I'd miss the biological pussy. I'm shooting my way
to suicide by cop.

Vietnam John is at the bar. Nothing like a grizzled vet at a bar
when you need to buy a gun. Of course, part of the price is that
you have to listen to whatever bullshit he's talking. If you need a
self-righteous old man who thinks he knows everything, find a
Vietnam vet. You never met a guy who hated combat more who
talks about nothing but killing.

. . . when you're recon, they drop you anywhere. And it's in the
complete fucking dark. Not regular dark, this is fuck-you dark. You
have to do that, or you'll be shot dead by the time you land. Well to
this god damn day I don't know what happened. I landed in a booby
trap or some shit. One minute I'm parachuting in, then my whole
world is pain, and then I wake up in someone's hut.

I was knocked unconscious, and by some fucking miracle, I wasn't hurt that bad. My legs and ankles were all jacked up and sprained, but nothing was broken. These villagers hadn't seen a white man before. I was a little farther behind the lines than was ever official. Hell, I'm not even saying I was in Nam for all it matters to you. Point is, this old broad is nursing me back to health, and I was the biggest thing to ever happen to this little piece-of-shit village.

Well this village is being terrorized by a fucking tiger. This tiger comes in whenever it feels like and kills their pigs and chickens like it's some kind of fucking buffet. Now that may not sound like much to you and me, but it's the literal life of these people. Slowly, the way they eat is being diminished. Still, they're bringing me bowl after bowl of homemade food. They can't do shit. They have one rifle, a .22 piece-of-shit, and a 410 bore shotgun that don't have no shells. But I have an M16.

That's why they're getting me healthy. That's why they're going hungry so I can eat. They've been praying for an answer, and then some dude falls from the sky covered in weapons? Yes, I was sent by God, and their food is tribute to God. If I get well enough, I figure it's my duty to whatever cosmic force that kept me alive to help these people.

When I get better, I live up to my end of the bargain. I know I'm going to find that fucking tiger and kill the fuck out of it.

So I set up a perch in a tree. I tie a few piglets to a stake in the middle of town. And I wait. And wait. And wait. Nothing. This stripy son of a bitch won't show his furry fucking ass for nothing.

Fuck it, you know, I get out of that fucking tree to go take a dump and get something to eat and see which one of these villagers wants to fuck her first white guy. As soon as I hit the ground, I hear nothing.

Hearing nothing is bad. The jungle is noisier than any city street. The jungle is as noisy as Manhattan. Monkeys and birds and all kinds of shit, a constant crowd of noises. Once you're in the jungle for a while, that shit is louder than a god damn parade.

When the jungle gets quiet, something is up. Shit got quiet because everything in this fucking jungle is afraid of this fucking tiger, and that tiger has to be right on top of me.

I look around. I can't see shit. But I know it sees me. I'm next. It's not looking at the piglets. It's looking right at me. The piglets aren't anything more than hors d'oeuvres compared to me. The whole jungle wants it to eat me. The jungle has nothing against me, but you know, better me than it, when it comes to getting eaten.

The ground raises up and hits me with six hundred pounds of force. I throw up from the movement—my insides just shoot out like stepping on a tube of toothpaste. Fucker waited till I turned around.

My M16 is gone; I'm looking at the insides of my backpack scattered about the ground in front of me. A flare gun. Better than nothing. I grab it, roll over, and I'm looking death in its fucking face, and it's all teeth and fur and tongue and hot spitty breath. This mouth just opens and gets bigger and fucking bigger. He's going to bite my head off.

I jam that flare gun into his mouth, down his throat, and pull the fucking trigger. Smoke and burnt hair, and he drops like fucking that. No matter what a badass he was on the outside, he was all soft and pink and flammable on the inside.

I'm lying underneath six hundred pounds of striped death, and I think, Holy shit, I can't breathe. I could suffocate under this son of a bitch. I'm squashed too flat to inhale.

The whole damn village comes and takes it off me. They watched the whole thing like it was the fucking Super Bowl. I'm fucked up from the whole thing, every last bit of adrenaline and endorphins emptied into my bloodstream. I'm shaking and numb. I'm covered in blood and piss and random liquids that came from inside the tiger.

They lead me down to the river, strip me, then wash me, all the while singing some song they all seem to know. Then they lead me back to the chief's hut.

So they bring me the village whore to fuck me, feed me all kinds of shit, and kids are making me things out of sticks and bamboo. One guy who actually has a job in the city tells me he's going to make a knife for me. Asking me all kinds of things about it. I don't speak what he speaks, but we both speak a little French. Or so I think.

I tried to ask him for a sixteen-inch knife. Sixteen is my lucky number, right? But I messed up something in the translation. He comes back with a sixteen-kilogram knife. Thirty-five fucking pounds. I had to get a backpack sheath made for this thing. The handle has this brass-knuckle-style grip around it. A lead-filled brass pommel the size of a fist. The blade is thick as an ax head at the top. And sharp. Hell.

Recon is about killing quietly. And this knife could kill a man before he felt it cut him. I could crush a man's skull with the dull end. Hell, I busted locks with that shit. Years later I opened coconuts with it, but that's another story. It was way too heavy for traditional knife fighting. But if I touched a guy with it and let the weight drop, I'd cut that fucker in half.

I brought it down on a man's shoulder once. His arm just popped off. He didn't even feel it. Just looked over at it, looked back at me, and fell over. Bled out. Shit. Went through anything and anyone. Some poor fucker tried to block it as it was coming down, and I cut his forearm off and it went right through his chest about halfway.

Man, I loved that fucking knife. Dropped it on my foot one day, and that was it for my service. Front half of my left foot was just gone. That knife kept me alive and sent me home . . .

I say, Hell of a story, John. I have to go see a man about a horse, and I'm going to need a gun.

You fucking kids. Letting history go by you.

I'm forty-three.

Still a fucking kid. You can still shit just like that. When you get older, you'll miss the days when the shit just flew right out of you.

I poop like I have a Swiss asshole, yes. Now, about the guns.

In the alley is a dirty van, a blue-and-gray custom that's seen better days. When John opens the door, there's a moment of freedom followed by a grip of wet dog stink. It's overwhelming. I'm trying not to look like I notice.

John enters the mouth of the horrible beast and returns with a duffel bag. He unzips it, takes out a folded towel. I recognize the towel. It's from the gym down the street in the Potrero Shopping Center. But it's stained and nasty, not like they'd want it back. John probably lives in his van and showers at the gym.

Three guns are laid out, from biggest to smallest, Goldilocks style.

This here is the .50-caliber Desert Eagle. Same shit Omar used in The Wire. *Ever since then, every wannabe gangster carries this. Now, if you can handle it, you can kill anyone with one shot. Hell, you can crack the engine block of a car with this. Only problem is, it's heavy and hard to use quickly.*

This is a SIG Sauer. Now this is a nice piece. For a little extra, I'll throw in some dumdums I have for it. CIA bullets that come out of the barrel end over end rather than spiraling. Less accurate, but if you hit a man in the arm, the bone will shatter. One hit anywhere, man's lucky he's alive.

And this last little fella is a .25-caliber Raven. Nice little guy. Six rounds. Nothing in the way of real stopping power, but hell, you shoot a guy, it'll take all the piss out of him. Better than nothing, and it's great in a knife fight. Easy to carry and conceal.

I used to have one like that. Where is it? What happened to it? It looks just like the one I had. I try to remember where it is, but it's like the memory is being erased as I access it. Wherever it is, looks like I need another. If I can't find it, it's of no use to me.

How much for the Raven?

Two hundred.

Steep.

Illegal.

You have a point. Throw in shells?

Of course.

You have a problem?

What?

I mean, do you have a problem I could help you with?

Nothing in particular . . .

It looks like you're flush. If there's a problem with a specific person, I could make that problem go away.

Nah, it's more of a preventative measure.

Well, keep me in mind if something specific comes up.

Back in the bar. Drinks. Lights drip and bleed. I'm coming down off something and coming on to something else. I'm an amusement park of drugs. More liquor. Black girl drinking Vanilla Stoli, she's pouring her own Cherry Coke in it. I try to order one. She laughs. I have no idea what I'm saying. Fuck I'm high. She slips me a pill. I take it.

You feelin' better, honey?

Yeah, that pill's working fine, took the edge off.

Glad to be of help.

Hey, did you see a guy in the ER who came in covered in shit?

Oh god, yes.

How's he doing?

The other nurses turn away. The laughter stops.

That ain't nothing to talk about right now.

I need to know . . .

Well, hell's bells. That boy got hosed off, and he had the nastiest gangrenous abscesses on both arms we'd ever seen over there. That's no bullshit either; we had to take pictures of them to show medical students.

Did you get him taken care of?

Aw, honey. We had to cut both his arms off. He was damn near dead. It was all that toxic shit in his blood that made him that crazy. If he hadn't come in when he did, he would have died in a few hours. The worst part . . . never mind.

Please.

No.

Please?

We had to do it without his permission. By the time he woke up, they were gone. He was still out of it. Asked me why he was strapped down. Motherfucker was still too high from the surgery to notice he didn't have arms. That's why he couldn't move 'em. Fuck. That's some real sad shit.

She drained her drink. I've worked bad jobs and weird jobs and I drank at them. I drank before and during jobs. But I've never really had a drive-me-to-drink job. Kind of the other way around with me. I kept jobs because I wanted to keep drinking. Two drunks, sitting next to each other, drinking in the early morning, couldn't be more different.

●

I have a graveyard full of dead friends. Once you hit forty, it's what happens. People die. It's not even tragic anymore.

When you were a teenager and that kid in your school died, it was a big deal. There was a page in the yearbook. You get high at a bonfire party and someone brings him up and someone cries and then everyone cries and there's making out and you feel horrible like the emptied bowels of a cow, but fuck, this might be the time you get laid, so there's that . . .

And in your twenties it happens, but it's almost beautiful, it's so tragic. You know a guy who died trying to climb a mountain. You know a guy who died in a bus in South America where he was doing Peace Corps work. There's the weird sudden cancer that takes someone far too young, WTF cancer. There's the OD of the guy who tried morphine during his semester abroad.

Then in your thirties, it's all fucked. That's when the bad ones go down. They found his body murdered, but he's a junkie so who gives a shit. They found her skull at a campground; she died hiking years ago. There was a bad batch of heroin with a flesh-eating virus. Motorcycle crackups. Drunk driving. Surfers caught in a riptide.

Forties, it's all old age, terminal disease, and suicides. Cancer. Suicide. Heart failure. Cancer. Pneumonia. Cancer. So much fucking cancer. All kinds. The slow kind that kills you over years, and the stomach pain that kills you in six months. Too late to quit smoking when you have four-months-to-live kind of cancer. People die, and you think, that's what old people die of, and you realize, yeah, I'm old.

But some of us won't die.

Those of us who never caught a break.

The one thing life handed us was some kind of freakish endurance. I've done twice as many drugs as other people who died from doing half as much. I've drunk enough to kill a man and snorted enough coke to kill another, and I call it Tuesday night. I've gotten away with it time after time, pushing myself as hard as I can, taking uppers when I'm down and downers when I'm up until I don't know which direction I'm facing at any moment. Hell, I don't need painkillers or speed; I need a fucking compass. I've gone into neighborhoods I shouldn't have been in, bought shit I was pretty sure was drugs from people I didn't know and smoked them with a pipe I made from garbage I found on the street, and I'm fine.

I should be dead, like a cockroach you step on and then lift up your foot and it runs off. It should be dead, and so should I.

Knew a guy named Tucson Sam—it was a play on Toucan Sam as far as I could figure, but he was actually from Phoenix or some shit. Sam had it all, or so I thought. He had a small-town handsomeness with a big-city mystery. He played guitar in a bunch of retro country bands. He had a great old truck that looked like it was out of a Norman Rockwell painting. The girls loved him, especially when he was heartbroken.

The more he got dumped, the more he got laid. One after another, they came to him, doe-eyed solutions to his problem. Now you should think at this point, why couldn't this fucker keep a woman around?

Along with everything else retro and cool about him in a rustic country way, he had a crippling problem with whiskey. He drank every day, and he only stopped to drink at night. That's why we were good friends. We drank together. I never told him to stop. I backed his play, listened to his troubles in the small moments between women.

He eventually wrecked the truck and got a motorcycle. The motorcycle was a rumbling blue ox to his rebellious Paul Bunyan. He looked like a biker, became a biker. Bikers liked him like women liked him. It was strange. He had this undeniable charisma. But as he dressed the part, he lived the part as well. Got into the drugs.

Bikers are famous for the speed, for the meth, but what they're really making their nut on now is Oxy. Too many people are cooking meth now, and it's too difficult to get the ingredients. Oxy is all made in a lab. No cookers to deal with, no lab explosions, no tweakers. And what they're selling, they're taking.

Sam got an Oxy habit. Which, like most Oxy habits, turned into a heroin habit. You remember drug week in high school? They always had this jag about marijuana being a gateway drug: smoke a joint, you'll have a needle in your arm by the end of the semester. Bullshit. Such bullshit. I think the first time you smoke a joint and don't try to fly off the roof of a skyscraper, you think everything you've ever been told is bullshit. So eventually you say fuck it, I'll try speed, and Vicodins and ecstasy and whatever people have. So drug week is the real gateway drug, right? That's what I thought until Oxy came around. Take it every day, and you will eventually end up shooting dope, I guarantee it.

Sam's heroin habit turned into psychosis. I don't know what really happened, but he lost his damn mind, is all I know. Lost his job, lost a bunch more after that, lost his bike, and worst of all, his looks. The girls stopped coming around. He had that look that junkies get that their face is one size too big for their skull. There's a strange gauntly gray sag they get.

The worst though is what he did to his dog. He killed his dog. Like butchered it, on the steps of the old bank that's now a social security office, on a Sunday morning in front of the brunch crowd outside of Boogaloos. They caught the whole thing on iPhones. Axed that fucker open. The cops were on him.

I hoped he'd get better. Maybe being locked up would do him some good, get him some help. But it did and it didn't help. It cleared up his mind, all right. But he couldn't live with what he'd done. He killed himself in a SRO in the Civic Center.

Poor guy. I used to think he had it made. I used to wish I were him. I wanted to be like him. That's the life of the junkie though. You don't know what it is until you're on that side.

There used to be this RV on Twenty-first Street. If you were desperate or dopesick, you could stick your hand in the hole with a ten-dollar bill, and someone on the other side would give you a tiny balloon of heroin.

On that same corner now is a food truck. If you are hungry or desperate, you can hand them a ten-dollar bill, and they'll hand you a kimchi burger. Much less of a deal, if you ask me.

I have to take the edge off. I feel like shit. My sweat's coming out in a slick film. My crotch is damp. My fingers are tingly. Loud. Everything is too loud—cell conversations, barking dogs, yelling children. Cars honking. Ring tones.

A woman in Lululemon gear ties her dog to a parking meter and heads inside the café. The dog cries, and I feel sorry for it. It has to live with her; it's codependent on her chronic abandonment. I know her type; I've worked the cafes before: she's the kind who asks for a drink, but everything about it is special needs: the temperature, the milk, the foam, the glass it's in ... nothing can be done for her like it's done for everyone else. She can't find one thing on the menu that she likes as is. Back in the day, we could just tell her no, to fuck off, that we weren't doing all that shit. But the new cafes ruined everyone. Which is my real beef with Starbucks. I don't care about corporate this and that. They indoctrinated the public into the coffee world. No one in America knew what a latte was until they came along. Starbucks became a place for all the fuckers with special needs to give directions and get attention. We used to ask for lattes and mochas in singles and doubles; now it's sizes. That's not how it should be done. We had a terminology that had existed for however long the espresso machine existed, and that place ruined it. I don't give a good god damn about the mythical mom-and-pop places, which are often owned by complete jerks who should be out of business. I'm against these marketing fuckers branding something that didn't need it.

Sunday mornings are hell in the Mission. It fills up with the brunch crowd that, if you don't live here, I can't really describe. Brunch is the disco of this decade. People wait in line for pastries at Tartine. Sure, it's good, I've been there on a weekday, but it's not stand-in-line-like-it's-Studio 54 good.

Mornings are hard on drug addicts. Shit is wearing off. Stuff we took two days ago is coming out of our systems, and we're coming down from stuff we took the day before. A call must be made: more of the same to keep the sickness away and the party rolling, or some assistance in the crash with something to take the edge off? A delicate balance must be maintained.

Some people see the drug life as easier, that you just get high and don't worry about shit. Not the case. The moment you buy your drugs, they start to run out. The more drugs you take, the more your tolerance grows, and therefore, you must buy more the next time. It's a tightrope act, with your emotions being the rope and drugs as the balancing pole. You fuckers on the ground do nothing, and you stay nothing. Not high, not coming down, nothing. I don't remember the last day I wasn't on something, coming off something, or recovering from something; usually it's a mix of all three in varying degrees, like three colors of light that sometimes, occasionally, when I get the mix right, burns a perfect pure white. Which makes it all worth it, and if you don't know about that, you'll never get it.

And you fuckers with your yoga mats and strollers and fair-trade toddlers crowd up my sidewalks and give me stares like I don't belong here. I'm here every day. Where are you? You're only here on the weekends. You're working down in Silicon Valley, leaving this street every day so you can afford to live here. You could take it easy and live in a van, like me. But you'll be paid off on that mortgage in another twenty-seven years when you're seventy. Maybe you'll like it here still. Maybe you'll be dead, and I'll be squatting in your house. How many purebred dogs will you go through in one lifetime? How many hybrid cars will you purchase? I hope you had a nice time with your life. I did stuff. I may end up with nothing, but we'll both be dead and it won't matter. We'll be on our deathbeds in the same room at SF General, and yeah you did CrossFit and yoga and ate gluten-free bagels, you had an IRA and a 401(k) and T-bills, whatever those are, and you dated respectable people and you married one and had two kids, one of each, and you raised them bilingual and sent them to good schools and you named them after your favorite characters in your favorite books that you read and you didn't watch TV because TV is bullshit, and me, I went into neighborhoods I shouldn't have been in and bought what I was pretty sure were drugs from people I didn't know and I smoked them from pipes I made out of garbage, and I didn't go to the dentist for the entirety of the '90s, and I ate meat, smoked, and wore leather, and I flushed the toilet whenever I fucking felt like it, fuck the drought and fuck the bad karma . . .

Chuck, bro, are you okay?

He's shaking me, a hand on each shoulder. I'm not wearing a shirt. Scratches like I fought a cat. Pants, no shoes. Barefoot on the sidewalk. The wind is cold; I'm covered in a thick sweat.

Chuck, we have to get out of here.

I know this guy. Can't place it. He's from another time, another life.

I'm in front of Tartine. The phones are out. I'm being filmed with iPads and cell phones. Nannies are shielding kids from me. Someone's yelling. Wait, it's me. I'm not thinking. I'm yelling.

Chuck, it's me, Eric. You are fucked up.

Eric's an old roommate. He lived in the pantry of my house on Laguna Street for a hundred bucks a month. Ninety. Ninety-one. Something. What year is it?

Eric tugs at me. I follow.

I'm at Eric's house. The walls are covered in rock posters and flyers. I'm sitting on a futon in the living room that's probably his bedroom as well. He tries talking to me, but the words are coming out so slowly I can't understand him. I'm falling in a remote hole.

Time pauses and restarts. A fly stops in front of me, hovers like a helicopter. It backs up, goes forward. This isn't good.

Eric comes back. He has a briefcase with him that's a stashbox. He opens it, rifles around, comes out with a tiny squeeze bottle. He tilts my head back and drops something liquid in my eye. It's cold. Then I feel good. And my cock gets hard immediately. I need to fuck somebody. Right now.

Ha, you like that, right?

Remote . . .

Oh shit, that's what this crash is. I have some of that. Hold on.

He rifles around some more. Finds a pill. He crushes it into a fine powder and holds it under my nose. I snort it like a drowning man grabbing for a rope.

What the fuck, Chuck?

What was that first shit you gave me?

Some new shit I'm fucking with. It's a failed antidepressant. It's supposed to turn depression into happiness, but it just crosswires sadness with sexual arousal. Of course, it never got through clinical trials. But it's the best ecstasy comedown cure ever. I'm running a weekend party the last week of every month. Sunday is comedown day. We show Hallmark commercials and montages from Old Yeller *and shit, and everyone gets naked and fucks. Even the ugly old guys like me. You should come. You're already halfway naked. Really though, what the fuck?*

Blacked out. Been taking a lot of shit. Speaking of which, I need to take a shit, a literal shit.

Down the hall. And take a shower. You smell fucking horrible.

The first shit blasts like a shotgun. Then nothing. Then it wells up again and blasts. Water and chunks. Then a stream of water, like a riot hose. Then nothing. I sit for a while.

Rock hard. Stroke. Think of Liza. What she used to look like. The Catholic schoolgirl uniform she showed off to you before you fucked her way back when. The event that led to the fetish. You're not interested in Catholic schoolgirls. You've been trying to fuck Liza again for years. Fuck her again. That's your thing with the skirt. You're chasing after her memory. Scars. Burns. No. Fuck. Think of that ass peeking from underneath the hem of the skirt. The first shaved pussy you'd ever seen. Only strippers and porn actresses had those then. It was the unshaven punk era. Shaven armpits were mainstream corporate bullshit. She's standing over you wearing a skirt with no panties and asking you what you think, and you're still afraid to make a move, frozen from a childhood of abuse and rejection. You can't say anything, and she laughs. *Take it out,* she says. She can see you're hard, you still harbor fear that she's going to laugh at it, but you take it out because that's what you're told to do. Instead of laughing, she hovers closer and closer, till she slides right on top of your cock and she's grinding you. A drop of sweat runs off her face and lands in your mouth. You don't want to come right away, but you do, a flush of heat ripping through your neck, you close your eyes . . .

You open your eyes. See the scars. Living room. Liza's here. Fucking Liza on the floor. Not a fantasy anymore.

Where am I?

What? Jesus, Chuck. You're in my living room.

I was just taking a shit in Eric's bathroom.

WHAT are you talking about? Shut up and keep fucking.

No, I was somewhere else.

You're high. Or not high enough. Here, take another hit.

She hands me the marble in a pipe and I hit it. I inhale and hold.

•

Shower water's hitting me.

I'm in Eric's bathroom.

Fuck, that felt real.

I look over. The bowl is disgustingly full. I reach out and flush.

There's nothing in this shower except for the peppermint Dr. Bronner's. I guess it'll have to do. I might stink too much for this. I need something stronger. Pine-Sol. Something.

I get out of the shower. Eric's waiting for me.

Take these sweats, this shirt, and these socks. I found your shoes and your jacket. Your shirt's gone somewhere. And your socks, well, fuck them. Totally gross. Basically you did a striptease at Tartine while you were blacking out.

Fucking hilarious.

Not really. This isn't the old Mission. This Mission belongs to the techies.

Bullshit.

Face it. They're here. They have money. That's how this country works.

Fuck it. I'm leaving anyway.

Listen. This isn't twenty years ago. You can't get away with anything you want anymore. You can't have a freakout like this. Dude, if I didn't live upstairs, you would've been arrested. And bro, you had a gun in your jacket, and god knows what in your system. They could've 5150'd you. Easily.

I know. Is my stash still there?

Fuck, really? That's what you're concerned about? Are you listening to me at all?

Christ, I just . . . is my stash still there?

No. Keys. And a little gun.

It's a Raven.

I don't care. Fuck. Dude, get your shit together, and get out of here.

Hey, sorry, I didn't mean to . . .

But you did. I'm trying to help you, and it's like you're in a different god damned world.

Sorry . . .

I'm sorry, too. I'm sorry for a lot of things. But it's not the good ol' days anymore, and frankly, I'm not sure that they even were good, ever. But one thing I know is that we're not twenty-one anymore. It's okay to be in our forties. We just have to act like it.

Okay, I'm leaving.

I get my things and wander instinctively toward the front door. As I open the door, Eric stops me and hands me a flyer. Some warehouse party off Third Street.

Show up. I'll put you on the list.

Thanks. I'll get these sweats back . . .

No worries, dude, he says, waving me off.

I lope down the steps and wander away, in the opposite direction of Tartine.

Where my van should be, it isn't. My mind shuffles. Did I move it? Did I drive it somewhere in a blackout? I don't remember, but hell, that doesn't mean a damn thing. Doesn't mean I did or didn't.

You looking for your van?

The voice startles me.

Over here.

A pile of garbage sticks an arm out and waves.

Yeah. Did you see what happened to it?

Got towed.

Towed?

Towed.

Ah, for the love of fuck.

Hey, got a quarter?

No. Especially not now.

Why?

You know why. They towed my van.

You have pockets.

You talk pretty bold for a pile of garbage.

Fuck you. I prefer refuse-American.

My money. My fucking money was in the van. I can't get the van out of the impound without them finding me, but I can't get to the money unless I do. Is this how they're trying to get me? Take my van and my money and wait for me to show up and then nab me?

Not me. Nope. They're not getting me that easy. No sir. They'll have to try something else. I'm not falling for that trap.

But I need money. I need drugs. I have to work something out. Someone has to front me.

By the time I get to the Tenderloin, I'm coming down again; I still have a hard-on, but it's not like it was.

Big Mike won't answer his buzzer. Calls go to voicemail; texts sit unread. Not good. He has a kitchen full of everything I need, but I can't get in.

There's a Crown Vic parked across the street. Undercover cops are common in the TL, but maybe they're watching Big Mike's place.

I can feel them looking at me, their eyes scanning the back of my neck, trying to look at the hands for telltale tats. I know they're behind that tinted glass checking me out. I have a sense for these things.

I scamper off, duck into the nearest corner store.

A smell hits me. It's a soured-cat-piss smell. The owner has his shirt pulled over his face. Looks helpless against it. I head back toward the beer. I know this smell, personally.

Oso's in the back of the store by the refrigerators.

Something's wrong. The man has lost a lot of weight. There's no way he could lose this much weight in what, a week and a half? His skin hangs loose on him like one of those Chinese fighting dogs. It creeps me out.

What you looking at, fool? he says with a sneer.

Oso, it's me, Chuck.

Oso squints. He walks toward me. He has a shopping basket filled with TV dinners, four or five ice creams, and a Desert Eagle.

Oh, shit, fool. What the fuck is up?

He smiles, but somehow it looks creepier than before. As he gets closer, I see tiny lumps under his skin.

You've lost some weight.

Funny. I'm smaller and shit. But I don't feel a god damn bit lighter.

You seen Big Mike around?

Nah. That fool is AWOL. Fucking up my business, that's for damn sure.

Aw, fuck.

What's up, fool?

I need something to tide me over. I lost my stash, my cash, and almost my ass.

I got your hookup. Come back to the crib and we'll work it out.

We walk out. Oso throws two twenties on the counter, doesn't stop to be rung up or wait for change.

In the studio, the smell is somehow worse than I remember. It throws me off balance. There's a taste in my throat; I'm afraid to breathe through my mouth, but when I breathe through my nose, it stings and burns. I'm not sure what's happening here. This is beyond rotten food or body odor or cats. This is something inhuman, something wrong, something that shouldn't be. There's some kind of strong ammonia theme that is making it hard for me to keep my eyes open.

Sit down, fool, Oso says.

I'm afraid to sit anywhere. It's really gross in here. I want to get some shit and leave. I want to go to rehab. I should quit all this shit. Not worth it. Not fucking worth it. I'll sell some drugs, get some money and go to rehab, then get out and get a square job.

I'll go to that rehab down south, Promises, I think it's called, the one where Robert Downey Jr. and Ben Affleck go, where you get clean by a pool, and I'll write a screenplay, and one of them will get it to their people, and then I'll have people waiting for me when I get out.

And I'll meet some nice actress from an old show like *The Facts of Life* or something who's having trouble with pills since her kid died or a car wreck or something, and we'll hit it off and she'll be tired of those Hollywood jerkoffs and want a real down-to-earth guy like me.

I wonder if Fairuza Balk will be there. I'll bet she has a drug problem. Look at those eyes, those crazy bright eyes—I bet you can see them in the dark like a cat. She's done some shit for sure. Haven't seen her in anything in a long-ass time; maybe she copped a habit and needs help.

We'll hang out when we're out and tell stories about when we were in there about how bad the food was and how fat one of the nurses was and how dumb the other actors were, and we'll laugh like we haven't laughed in so long and she'll say, *You know, I haven't laughed like this in forever*, and I'll say, *Me neither*, and she'll say, *You look really good, you have some color back in your face and you put some meat on you*, and I'll be like, *Thanks, I've been working out, and your skin looks great*, and she'll say, *Thanks*, and there will be this pause where we both try to take drinks of our raw-food juices but they're empty and then we both go to say something then we both stop and then say, *No you go*, at the same time and then we'll laugh and then she'll say, *Have you ever been to the Hollywood Forever Cemetery?* and I'll be like, *No what's that?* even though I know what it is, and she'll say, *It's this cemetery and they show old horror films there and tonight they're showing* Night of the Living Dead *and we should go*, and I'll be like, *Hell yeah*, and we just hang out till then and everything's cool till right when the movie starts and she just fucking gets on me and kisses me and looks at me with those crazy eyes and that's how we fall in love, you know, and *It's weird*, I'll say, and *What?* she will ask, *What's weird?* and I'll say, *We never would've met if we hadn't gotten strung out and that rehab was the best thing that ever happened to me*, and she'll giggle and say, *Me too*, wipe a little tear out of her eye, and make out with me for the rest of the movie.

Chuck?

What?

You here?

Yeah.

Good. I'm going to front you some more of these marbles. Having a hard time moving them with that high retail and all. You move those okay?

Yeah, I know some high rollers.

Okay, I'll give you eight for five.

I need forty grand.

Why? he says with a laugh.

I'm going to rehab.

Oh, you're going to reeeeeeehab. La-di-da. Well, it's a good place to meet future customers.

No, really. I'm going to get clean. Get off this hamster wheel.

Yeah right.

Don't get me wrong, I'll keep selling. Just won't pinch off my supply anymore.

Now you're talking. Anything else you need?

Um, a vial of remote, an eightball of coke . . . what about the forty grand?

I can't spare that much shit. You're going to have to sell a hundred wholesale to make forty yourself. You want to branch out maybe? Man, I got a brick of meth I can't do shit with.

Me neither. That market's too weird. I don't want to sell to anyone who likes doing that shit. Fucking tweakers.

Chuck, I've known you a long time, fool. Don't make me regret fronting you all this shit. Fuck, if Big Mike were still around, this wouldn't be happening. But I'm behind. I got bills, too.

I gather up the drugs and head for the door.

Seriously, Chuck, if I don't see you within a week, I'm getting someone to take care of this for me.

●

I stop in what used to be a grand foyer. Now it's a trashed entryway in a Tenderloin apartment building. This whole neighborhood used to be a grand place. It was theaters and upscale apartments. This was the place to be. Now it's a sinkhole for the least-welcome San Franciscans. It's the hair-and-cum-clogged drain hole of the city. Maybe of the state—hell, the western US. The whole city is squeegee-mopped into this tiny shit triangle.

No one cares what happens down here. There's a swarm of cops on the street, but they're just there for the fallen bodies. You can be loud and crazy and none of your neighbors will give a shit, you can walk down the street in only your pajama bottoms and no one will say a thing, you can be smelly and messy and dirty and you're not the worst one you'll run into that day. And you can do coke in the foyer of a Tenderloin building and no one, if they notice, gives a shit.

Two eyes of remote and a healthy snort of coke and I'm feeling all right. Cold rush of Tenderloin air hits me in the face like a damp towel that's been reused too many times—it smells a little, but it's a vast improvement over where I've been. Sun's on its way down, and Turk Street is waking up.

Two junkies are fighting over a glove. Each one has a glove and claims the other stole the other glove. This is the kind of thing that matters down here. This is what you get stabbed over, what you get a brick in the back of the head over, what gets you pushed in front of the 27 Bryant.

It's *Fuck you no fuck you motherfucker* back and forth in a rhythm that's native to this neighborhood but doesn't exist in music or poetry. It's the percussion of wingnut aggression.

I walk downhill toward Market Street. This day isn't so bad. Tonight there may be something to get into. What day is it? Sunday? Yes, it should be Sunday. I need to find Liza, sell her some of this shit, get some cash, and get started over. Hell, I need a place to stay. I don't have any money, but I have drugs. And like the saying goes, drugs will get you through times of no money better than money will get you through times of no drugs.

Liza's not picking up. I don't know where she is. I'm not getting the money or a place to stay. Fuck it. Who needs sleep? I have fucking drugs. I'll just stay up all night.

The problem with this is that one still needs a place to go when staying up all night with no money. I can't wait in a bar or go to the Lucky Penny with no money. If I get high enough to stay up all night, I'm not going to want to sit somewhere, staring at the sidewalk.

That's when I spot the old Rialto. It's a movie theater on Market Street that shut down in the early '90s. It was a real shithole. The last theater you could smoke in. Smoking was allowed on the balcony. It got weird up there, though. A lot of crack-smoking went on up there. Crackheads think everyone who's not smoking with them is a cop. No matter what you look like, they will make you for an undercover, which is not cool.

The Rialto had all-day tickets, so a lot of guys would get a ticket just to sit and drink, sleep maybe. If you got in early, you could stay for about twelve hours. Twelve hours out of the elements with a place to shit is valuable when you're living on the street.

This one time I was in there, a hooker came by. I have no idea what she looked like; she was just a silhouette to me. I thought she was trying to get by in the aisle. *You looking for a date?* she asked. I had no idea what that meant. I was still green enough to think that a date was when you picked up a girl at her house. I was like, *What?* and she repeated it, like, *Are you LOOKING for A DATE?* Then I got it. I told her no, and she growled at me. *What kind of FAGGOT are you?* Then one of the bums sleeping there yelled back, *HEY SOME PEOPLE ARE TRYING TO FUCKING SLEEP HERE.* That's the San Francisco I remember.

It's a far fucking cry from that to Foreign Cinema. To fucking mommy-and-me noon movies. To stadium seating and pre-picked seating and full bars at the Kabuki. People complain about gentrification. Do you want the smoke-filled movie theaters that smell like chlorine and crack smoke, with broken seats and sticky floors, the theaters you're afraid to fall asleep in, that someone may rob you? Frankly, I'm not sure which I liked more.

But back to the point. This used to be a shithole theater. Now it's a squat, run by my old punk pal, Claw.

Claw is a punk with a natural-gray Mohawk. Looks way older than the forty-nine that he is. In punk years, that's four years past dead. So hell, that he's still kicking is an achievement.

Down the alley. No lights. Bang on the door.

Dumpster lid opens with a bang. Punk pops his head up like a jack-in-the-box with matted dreadlocks.

What you want, yuppie?

I'm no yuppie, you summer runaway. I fucked your mom in that Dumpster before you were born.

Fuck you, asshole, I'm going to cut you into rat-sized bites.

I have drugs and I'm here to see Claw.

Why didn't you say so, fuckwad?

The kid turns on a walkie-talkie. Talks squatter code into it. The squatters have their own lingo and symbols. What looks like graffiti to you and me looks like instructions and information to them. It's a holdover from hobo culture.

If you see an abandoned building in the city, there's likely tags on it squatters can read. Stuff about how to get in, what kind of place it is, who lives there, that kind of thing. One symbol means infested with rats, another means working electricity, and another means vegans only. Some will tell you that door isn't really locked or which window you can crawl into.

Same with Dumpsters. There are markings about when to dive it and what's in it. There are marks that tell you when the employees dump everything and what kind of food it is. Donuts every four hours, 12:00, 4:00, 8:00. One day expired meat, dairy, and cheese 3:00 AM.

If you're hungry or don't have a place to sleep in San Francisco, you're doing something wrong. If you're smart enough, you have plenty of both. Maybe you're too fucked up to keep track of it, maybe you're too proud or picky to eat out of the trash, maybe you've softened yourself with housie life too long to sleep on cardboard, but if you're willing to do what it takes, you'll be fine.

A fire escape falls to the ground. It's badly rusted, well past twenty years of needing repair. Small chunks are missing; there are bent places that have been vainly restraightened. It's not fixed so much as it's been unbroken. It's to a point of working, but nowhere near safe. But I grab on nonetheless and make my way up.

The first room inside is an old office. It's barely lit, but it smells like it's full of punks. That old-sock-and-cigarettes smell.

A bunch of kids huddle over something with a pair of pliers. Stuffing flies out over their shoulders. As I walk by, I see they're tearing apart a Teddy Ruxpin doll. Not sure why, and I don't want to know. Probably trying to make a tattoo gun.

I walk through to the main hallway, getting mad-dog stares from the newer ones and ignored by the veterans. The fresh ones give you a look that says you don't belong here, but the old hands at this make you feel like you don't even exist. You're not worthy of being noticed. You're invisible unless you're one of us, that kind of thing.

I leave through a hallway, home to a gaggle of aging crusties. It's impossible to determine their age. Street kids age in harsh curves of degradation. They look fine until they don't. Their teeth are fine until they all go bad at once. Their skin is fine until one day it looks like a CPR dummy's covering. It's more about mileage than years.

Where's Claw? I ask, and they point to a theater door without saying a word or looking up. I think I recognize one of them, but I mean, what the fuck do I have to say to any of them at this point? I'm on a mission, a mission from drugs.

Point Break is on. They only have a handful of films that were out at the time the theater went down. It's ragged, been spliced together many times, the audio is shit, but it's working.

At the front of the theater, a small crew acts out the movie, *Rocky Horror* style. It's more than entertainment for them. It's a way of life.

Once you reject everything in your life, when you've thrown out your family's religion then rid yourself of all other traditional religions, seen through the empty promises of vague spiritualities, become bored by all the God-talk of atheists, despise the lack of commitment of agnostics, there's still a hole that needs to be filled.

Some people fill it with work or ambition or raising kids or building Harleys. But if you have none of these things, have severed connections with owning things or being close with another person, there's all this time to fill.

Sure, there's drugs and sex and loud music, but they only frame the hole; they don't fill it. Getting high and fucking and listening to your favorite band are more fun when it's with something or someone who means something to you.

Most people don't have time to think about this—literally, they don't have the time, because we spend so much time at work or getting somewhere or getting ready to go somewhere. But when you really have that grand amount of time that squatters have, you end up with a spiritual problem. You have a lot of time to focus on that nothing really matters since the human race goes extinct at some point and the earth doesn't stop spinning unless the universe contracts on itself.

It may be pointless to dedicate yourself to live reenactments of *Point Break*, *House Party*, and *Blind Fury*, but is it really any less meaningful than going to a bank job every day so you can pay for stuff you don't need that you also don't have time to enjoy?

In the back, where the chairs used to be, are a herd of discarded couches. Couches are horrifyingly expensive to buy but almost impossible to get rid of. No one wants used couches, but people are more than willing to spend thousands on a new one. Where do they go? Landfills, mostly, but also squats like these.

Claw reclines on a silver-duct-taped couch that I think used to be covered in black leather. He's wearing the same damn shit he wore in the early '90s, only he's a little fatter and has gone completely gray in the Mohawk. It's a sign of respect around here, a sign that he's never sold out, that he's stayed true to his intentions of living outside the system but inside the city.

Chuck? What brings you out of the land of the homebound?

The law. I stole some shit.

Nice. Did you bring any to share?

Not that kind of thing. I do have some things to share, however.

Money or drugs?

Drugs.

No meth. We had a bad run of tweakers here. I can't really keep squatters from tweaking, but I don't want any more of that shit here than I have to have.

I have something you'll like.

I show him a marble.

The fuck is this? he says, rolling it in his fingers.

I take out a pipe and a lighter.

Let's find out.

We pass it back and forth, watching Keanu and Patrick banter back and forth. Whatever happened to Lori Petty? There were so many tank girls out there after her movie. The look took over for a summer.

How many hits do you get out of this thing?

No one knows; it doesn't really seem to run out.

Bullshit. It has to run out eventually. Or go bad or something. How much?

A thousand.

Fuuuuuuuuuck, Chuck.

Over time, it's not a bad deal.

You have a point.

Claw calls in his walkie-talkie. We wait, still smoking.

A rope drops from the ceiling. A kid dressed like a ninja slides down it, drops a backpack in front of us, then runs up the aisle.

What the fuck was that? I say with a laugh.

Your pay.

I pick up the backpack, unzip it, and look inside. A thousand dollars in ones—dirty, wrinkled ones bound with rubber bands that smell like wilted lettuce. I guess I'm lucky that it's not in pennies.

When I wake up, *Kindergarten Cop* is playing.

There's a strange smell of burnt plastic, almost crack smoke, but a little different. Maybe it's burning plastic. Fuck, I need to get out of here.

The backpack is gone.

Fuck fuck fuck panic fuck freak out.

Different clothes. Wearing different clothes. Calm the fuck down. Something's wrong. But you're okay.

Tattoos gone. That's not right. There should be tattoos on your forearm.

Dream. Dreaming. Yes. Let it ride. Like the Mission Street dream.

Wait. I was here. Before. Here. These clothes. This theater.

I went to see *Total Recall* with Jessica. We had a fight. I went to the other theater and drank. I passed out. Next thing I knew, I was at home. Jessica wouldn't return my calls. She dumped me. Never knew why.

I'd see her around now and then—from across the street, and she'd look the other way. She left a party when she saw me walk in. Then she moved to Portland. Then bounced around. Ukiah. Eugene. I didn't hear from or about her for a long time until I heard she cracked up riding a Harley with her girlfriend on the 101.

Fuck. What is going on?

I don't remember this part of the movie. I guess my brain is making it up as it goes. I'm curious but more curious about something else.

I walk out of *Kindergarten Cop*. *Total Recall* is playing next door. The smell of BO and lunchmeat hits me as I enter. Cigarettes, popcorn, and Pine-Sol. There's a soda pop stain on the screen; it looks like a horrible birthmark when it lands just right on the actors.

Jessica's here. I recognize her dreadlocked silhouette easily. I walk to the seat next to her . . .

Jessica?

You're such an asshole.

I know. I'm sorry.

Sorry's not enough.

I just want to make things right.

You say that but you don't mean it. You never mean it.

I don't understand. I don't know what's wrong.

Are you not paying attention to any fucking thing I say?

Look, I'm a little bit high, why don't you tell me again.

I can't believe I'm doing this. Okay. I told you I was pregnant, and you said, and I quote, "That sucks."

That's what it was. I had gotten her pregnant. I probably said it sucks about something in the movie, or a trailer or something. I don't remember her saying that. No wonder. I don't blame her one fucking bit for not speaking to me.

I'm sorry. I didn't mean "that sucks" about you being . . .

SHUT UP, a man yells at us. He stands up a couple of rows in front of us and turns around. He just keeps standing up. He's a mountain.

You shut the fuck up, she spits at him.

Not cool. Not cool, Jess. Fuck.

The mountain crawls over the horizon line of seats, one row at a time. As big as he is, he was farther away than I thought. He gets bigger as he climbs over each row. A Grimace-shaped mound of flesh coming at us . . .

Oh, what are you going to do? Come back here and whup our asses? My boyfriend knows karate, asshole.

Fuck. I do not.

Flesh mountain is right in front of us and picks me up with one hand in my armpit, the other hand on my neck. I'm off the ground. I can't breathe.

Karate this, motherfucker, he says, and he squeezes. I'm looking at Arnold on the screen. He's losing air on the unprotected surface of Mars. His eyes bulge, his lungs empty . . . I'm out.

I wake up. I'm on the duct-taped couch. My backpack is still there. My shoes, however, are gone. Fucking squatters. I smoke up and bail. I have shoes to buy.

THE MONSTERS ARE LOOSE ON MISSION STREET

I'M IN THE Mission breaking in my new Adidases and making my way up to Liza's place, past the vegan burrito place across from Taqueria Murder—well, we call it that because some gangland shit went down in there in 1990. The vegan place is Gracias Madre, a horrible entryway into gentrified San Francisco.

The really insulting gentrification is the replacement of established businesses with yuppie replicas. The genuine barbeque places on Divisadero are shut down and made into yoga studios, and in the Lower Haight, the ironic barbeque place opens. The old-man barbershops are shut down and vintage clothing stores open, and later, the old-timey barbershop opens. When the cycle gets fast enough, the new-school fake Mexican food place opens across the street from the real one. The only hope is that the real one beats the fake one. In the end, gentrification comes down to who owns the building and who will pay more to rent the spaces. Even though it makes money, the taqueria will eventually disappear from the mission because the real estate doesn't make sense. We'll always have a Mission-style burrito, but it won't be the same.

Something's awry on Mission Street; there's something going on. The hipsters are moving toward Valencia, and the junkies are moving toward Sixteenth. The crazy guy who plays Hacky Sack with old beer cans scampers off and disappears down Clarion Alley. The old white guy who wears basketball jerseys and screams random shit about being in the penitentiary disappears behind a door. Motherfuckers are running.

I should run, too, but I'm too high. My inertia keeps me going down to the corner of Nineteenth. I keep looking down there—is it a fire, a wreck, a drive-by? In the late '80s and early '90s, shit went down around here as the Norteños and Sureños got in an all-out war over the control of Twentieth Street. Nobody won. Honda Civics poked out Uzi snouts and sprayed at pay phones where *vatos* stood ground with pagers. Twenty years later, it's still neutral ground.

The adrenaline's flowing, but my blood feels thick, like hot fudge going through my veins. I'm floating down Mission. As the chaos increases, everything seems to calm for me. I see people screaming but I can't hear them. All I hear is the Five Stairsteps singing *Oooh child things are going to get easier, ooh child things'll get brighter*... A Latino mom runs by, carrying her child like a football, his mouth open in a scream I can't hear. A pudgy hipster in cutoff skinny jeans has lost his sense of irony; he jumps and scatters his way through the street between cars ... It's a social clusterfuck down here, and I couldn't be more at home.

NSA Andy runs up the street in a hospital gown, torn and hanging on like the flag of a defeated army, somehow. His head is freshly shaved, and his eyes are big as Skoal cans. Where each arm used to be is a stump with crossed *X*'s of stitching. He's screaming the *Gilligan's Island* song at full screech, no, *Petticoat Junction*. Wait, both.

Andy's lost it, for real. I don't think he knows where he is. Maybe he's stuck in a bad dream, running down Mission street in an unending night terror, running from NSA agents, CIA spooks, FBI assassins, Greenpeace hit men, white-power survivalists, black panthers, tenderloin crack dealers, old bosses, the babysitter who molested him, all of his demons real and imagined, those from his past and those who never existed.

His eyes lock with mine, and the world tunnels into his face. He recognizes me, a friendly face in the crowd of chaos and mayhem. He smiles a desperate smile, distorted by his freakishly bulging cheeks. The distance between us closes until we are inches apart. The song stops.

Fix me, he says, opening his mouth.

I think he's talking about his arms. A speech coils in my brain; I want to think of what to say, how to explain his arms to him, but then the junkie in me registers what's going on.

Tiny balloons are held chipmunk-style in his cheeks. Someone gave this man a mouth full of dope. Some heroin dealer took mercy on him, out of kindness or abject fear, and gave Andy a week's worth of dope. Problem is, how the hell is he going to shoot up? A monkey could fix with his feet, and a junkie could find a vein in a bowling ball, but this poor drug fiend is fucked as fucked can be. All this dope and no way to shoot it.

Aw, brother, I say, *I ain't got no works on me. Just a pipe.*

They took my arms.

I know.

They were going to take my legs next.

Now, I don't think . . .

They were going to cut me away until I was a brain in a jar, forever trapped in a dream, stuck in my own thoughts and never waking, on the shelf of an NSA freak like a trophy.

Sirens that sound off a Frankie Goes to Hollywood song. *Relax. Don't do it . . .*

They're coming for you Andy. You need to get out of here.

Andy looks around.

Capp Street, I tell him. Go down Capp Street. If there's one place in the world you may not stick out, it's there.

Andy runs. It's a panicked fear that fuels him in a PCP-like fury. Cars screech and stop. The frightened villagers spread out, running from this monster that's come down off Potrero Hill in seek of . . . well, this monster just wants to get high. He just needs a friendly hand and a rig.

BACK AT LIZA'S

FUCK, SHE SAYS, you smell. Like bad, like fuck it.

Good to see you, too.

Come in. Get out of those clothes and in the shower.

I walk down the hallway, dropping clothes as I go. I can smell myself. It must be really bad. It's like an old lunch in the fridge that you can't smell until you open it. Both metaphorically and literally. I smell like an old lunch, a half-eaten sandwich with some kind of oil or dressing that turned.

I line up my drugs on the bathroom counter. Coke, remote, a marble, and a pipe. I turn on the water, let the hot water steam up the room a bit. I take a bit of each. A small bump of coke for each nostril. Just enough remote to keep things normal. A long, healthy marble hit.

The water takes off a layer of funk. It's right about to scald but just a tiny bit tolerable. I slow everything down and let it sink in.

In what feels like hours, Liza walks in, naked.

Drugs! she squeals. *They're my FAVORITE. However did you know?*

Liza hoovers the coke. Christ, she can disappear that shit up her face hole. She takes a full dose of remote, but when she sets it down, she knocks it over.

FUCK. Liza!

Jeez, I'm sorry. I'll get you more.

Fuck. I was all set. That was my personal stash.

Did you fuck around and get a habit?

What the fuck do you think? I've been hooked on that shit for months.

Well, let's get you cleaned up and get you some more. I know a guy.

She takes a giant marble hit. That, she's welcome to. She can smoke all of that shit she wants.

My guy will probably want some of these, too. He has money. Cash. Lots of money.

That's my girl. Now put the pipe down and get in here.

Like every good drug addict would, she takes one more hit. She sets down the pipe and gets in the shower.

Faded tattoos, some well done and some fucked from the get-go, cover her body like stickers on a guitar case. She has scars she can't remember the start of, piercings so old she's forgotten about them. She's missing an ear, an eye, and a lot of her scalp, but still, she's a beautiful lady, more than what I deserve.

THE GUY

WE'RE IN FRONT of a warehouse somewhere off Third Street. I never figured this neighborhood out. It's an industrial area, one of the few areas of town that hasn't been made into a cute or up-and-coming area. It's still warehouses and cab companies and the occasional rave.

The warehouse used to be a bottling company; you can still make out the lettering on the side of the building. But the colored lights coming out of the top row of windows are a dead giveaway, as are the beats quietly thumping bass notes. What used to be a blue-collar warehouse is now a drug and party palace.

I stay close behind Liza. She's decked out like a sad doll. Sort of goth, but she looks more like a toy, like a Raggedy Ann, but sad. A permanent frown done with makeup to look like it's sewn on.

This is the place Eric was talking about. I can tell when we walk in. It looks like the receiving room of a funeral home, but with house music. There are the steampunks and the goths, the hipsters and the cool, and voyeurs scattered about who don't quite know what's going on. People are crying and feeling each other up, slight groping, like a family funeral with hugs that linger a bit to long and have maybe more hip grindage than you would want from your aunt.

We cut through the room to a hallway. It's lined with movie posters. They're going to be showing *Bicycle Thieves*, *Where The Red Fern Grows*, and *Old Yeller*. *The Champ* remake with Ricky Schroder. *The Outsiders*. *Never Let Me Go*. *Grave of the Fireflies*. Then there's the remixes, the three suicide scenes from the three

A Star Is Born movies, the death scenes from the *Rocky* movies, and one that seems to be really popular, the Disney Death Film, a montage of all the cartoon characters from Bambi's mom to Simba's dad that die in the various animation features, plus a sequence of Wile E. Coyote dying over and over.

There's a line of furverts waiting to get into that one. Plushies. They're dressed in anthropomorphic animal costumes. They will pile up in there and furry fuck each other, some rubbing off on the other costumes, the others with action flaps that lift up and allow for actual fucking. It's a super sweaty mess of fat-people BO and jizz in there in no time; those costumes are hot inside. Hell, I can't fuck with a shirt on without feeling constricted and dangerously heated. I have no idea how they get it on dressed like a giant bunny.

There's a sample in the house music, Erik Satie mashups. Then comes Pachelbel's Canon in D. Albinoni's Adagio in G. Old music with sad new beats. "Eleanor Rigby" chunks played in loops. Procol Harum's "A Whiter Shade of Pale." Music that makes you sad on a great day.

We walk up the stairs and through a floor that has a *Giving Tree* theme. That sad fucking book about codependency and enabling. It's a horribly sad book, and I don't know why it's ever given to a child. Fucking greedy bastard in the book takes every-thing from the tree until it's a stump and then sits on what's left. What kind of message is that? The tree should've eaten that fucker.

There's a poetry reading happening, and we move our way through that as fast as we can. All poems about dead mothers and cancer and lost loves and needless suicide. There's a group called the Sylvia Plath Hallelujah Chorus that's going to perform later, and I definitely don't want to be around for it. There's a giant oven set piece that they all walk into in the end.

We make our way to a third-floor room, through a series of soundproofed doors. Finally, we're about to meet the guy. The guy. Her guy. It's always the guy. Like a drug version of a Paul Reiser joke. He was joking about getting the TV fixed or some shit, but it works with the drug world as well. There's always A GUY.

By the last door is a hulk of a man, a cartoony figure in his bulk. I recognize him from the gym where Big Mike and I sold the horsemeat. Away from the other monstrous men, he looks somehow bigger. Standing by a normal door, he looks like a joke. His pupils are pinned. He's high as hell on something, and I'd rather not find out what.

We walk up to him. He stares at us like he can't see us. Like a blind man's dead-eyed stare.

Cecil? Liza says.

The hulk stares. Doesn't move. I'm high, the lighting's weird, but now I'm doubting whether or not he's alive. He's dead or some kind of statue. I look around. There's a camera above him.

The door clicks open. Hulk man stands aside enough for us to enter.

The inside of the room looks like the model for a condo. It's a studio apartment, decked out with new furniture.

Cecil, aka THE GUY, sits on a couch in front of a coffee table. He's watching TVs. Not TV. There's a wall of them with the sound down and the closed-captioning on. His eyes dart from one screen to another. He waves us in and asks us to sit. He gives us the one-minute finger.

There's a basket of identical remotes in front of him. He picks up one with a number 19 written on it and clicks one TV off. Then he looks at us, adding us into a rotation of the twenty TVs he has in the room.

I have some great stuff, he says. *I can split my attention to multiple sources and never get distracted. The more I take, the more things I can watch. I watched all of Martin Scorsese's movies at the same time. What a rush. What can I do for you, Liza?*

We need some remote. I wanted to get it from you so we can be sure of the quality.

I have dozens of dealers in here I can hook you up with.

There's something else.

What?

My boyfriend Chuck has some new shit that he needs an outlet for.

Well, is that so, Boyfriend Chuck? I see new shit in here every week. I have new shit like some clubs have new bands. I don't care about shit because it's new. I care about it because it's great. Not good, great. Is your new shit great, Boyfriend Chuck?

Yes, I say. *It's great stuff.*

I take the marbles out and put them on the table. He squints at them, then looks at me. His mouth tightens.

I've seen this shit before, he says, anger rising in his voice. *Get it the fuck out of my sight.*

No, it's new, it's good, I swear.

Do you know what it is?

Yes. Well, no, but it's great stuff.

You're not using it, are you?

Yeah.

You've done it more than a couple of times?

Yeah. It's good. I swear. The high is clean, the crash self-manages.

I don't know how to tell you this.

What?

We call it black hole. You need to stop doing this shit now. Right now. We call it black hole because it sucks you into itself and there's no way out. And it's black and round, but that's a nice coincidence. Get rid of it. I don't care how. Throw it in the ocean, bury it, drop it in acid. Whatever it takes. But stop taking this. Take anything else. Pick up a heroin habit, for fuck's sake. You god damn kids. Stick with the classics: heroin, cocaine, Oxy, sure, you'll get strung out but it won't completely fuck up your sense of reality.

I turn to get Liza's opinion.

She's gone.

Chuck? Cecil asks, snapping his fingers. *You with me, buddy?*

Liza, I say. *I was looking for Liza.*

Cecil looks at me quizzically. He rummages through his desk drawer and comes out with a wristband. He holds it up. I put out my wrist.

Suit yourself, he says. He fastens it on. *I can't see how it will help, but it can't hurt, I guess.* He looks to the hulk. *Ismail, take him down to the Liza room.*

The hulk comes over to lead me away. Liza has her own room here? I'm not sure what's happening. I just go with the flow. I follow the hulk to an elevator. We get in. There are buttons with no numbers on them. It shakes, jumps—it's an old freight elevator with blinking Christmas lights all over it. I can't tell if we're going up or down. It is as bumpy as a stagecoach ride.

When we stop, he pulls the door open. I see a hallway.

Which way?

He pushes me out of the elevator and shuts the door. There are anonymous doors, locked, with aging knobs, losing their color. Until I come to a door that's marked: "Living Inquiry, Zygotic Android" Project. LIZA. Fuck. This isn't what I meant.

I go back to the elevator. Push the button. Nothing. I push it more. Nothing. It's not responding. This hallway is all locked doors and the LIZA room. Maybe that's the way out. Someone must be there.

The LIZA door is locked as well, but the knob is new. I jiggle the knob and hear a beeping sound followed by the door unlocking. There's a reader on the door somewhere activated by the wristband.

The door opens into a locker room. It's all white tiles and lockers with black locks on them. There's a laundry basket holding a solitary container with a screw-on cap in the middle of the floor.

Chuck? a voice says over the system. I look around. I don't see anyone. I do spot a speaker in the ceiling. *Chuck, please disrobe and put your personal belongings in the basket. Leave a urine sample. Then continue through the showers. Bathe thoroughly. Even if you don't think you need it.*

I take off everything. I can smell myself, a particularly bad BO. I had no idea. This place smells so neutral that my smell is louder than a laugh in a library. I put everything in the basket, pee in the sample jar, and walk through the showers.

There are no fixtures, only a digital display. It blinks on and flashes *STEAM* repeatedly.

Steam starts from jets along my entire height. It's right at the temperature that borders on feeling great and scalding. Right as I'm getting lightheaded, it stops. The display blinks *SOAP. CLOSE EYES.*

I close my eyes and get a steady stream of soap sprayed on me. This is a human fucking car wash.

The soap is followed by a rinse cycle. The stream is just a little less solid than a fire hose.

The shower stops. *Proceed to the next room,* the voice says.

The door at the end of the shower room has no knob. It has a small hole with a graphic of a hand with the index finger extended. I slip my index finger inside it. Sharp pain, and I withdraw.

There's a tiny hole. These fuckers took a blood sample. The door clicks open.

There's a room with a white floor, ceiling, and walls, and nine silver pods. One is open, and the hulk is there, looking impatient. He motions to me, and as I walk closer, I see he wants me to get in.

Deprivation tanks. This isn't my thing. I like the drug highs, not organic highs. This is for people using orgone accumulators, dream machines, and the like. The "you don't need drugs to get high" assholes. Fuck that.

Hey, Ismail, that's your name, right? These tanks, not my thing. There's been a misunderstanding. I was looking for a lady named Liza, not a whatever this is.

Ismail still isn't in the mood to talk. He motions for me to enter the tank.

If it's all the same to you, I'll just take my clothes back and get the fuck out of here, better for having a shower.

Ismail does nothing. I do nothing. His expression worsens. I do nothing. He contorts my wrist in a way that hurts down to my feet. I try to squirm away, but I end up in the tank.

It's filled not with water, like I expect, but a warm gel, a little less thick than Jell-O. There's some kind of minty tingling that's really nice. I sink in until I'm suspended completely, with only my face above the gel.

Ismail bends over and pinches my nose shut, forcing my mouth open, and he sprays something into my throat. It comes on like Chloraseptic, cherry flavored, but I can taste something else in there. A psychedelic.

The lid closes over me. I would try to fight my way out, but I know better. I'm much better off riding out a psychedelic trip than trying to escape.

Time is perception more than space. Sure, things seem big when they're not; you remember your childhood home as a gargantuan building and when you see it as an adult, it's a two-bedroom shack. There's also body dysmorphia, where anorexics think they're fat and enormous bodybuilders think they're scrawny. But what I'm talking about is how you perceive time passing.

You think you know how long it's been between events, but you measure them by a number of other events happening. You don't actually feel the time pass. You feel the temperature of the day change. A movie seems short or long by how well the events are written. The ice in your glass melts. But take away the outside stimulus, all light and touch and taste and sound and smell, and your sense of time disappears. The way you think of time is only a sensory collage.

Thus the deprivation tank. Take the senses away, and you're left with a blind grasp at time.

Chuck? The voice from the intercom has returned. *Relax. The LIZA procedure will begin soon. You likely won't notice a thing.*

It will feel like a long dream. Your responses to the stimulus will be recorded for use for playback with our androids later. All of us at the LIZA project are extremely grateful for your volunteering. We would also like to let you know that you have tested positive for herpes. Upon completion of the exercise, we also recommend you have treatment for your liver and pancreas. Thank you.

I'm floating above the earth, but I don't dare turn around. If I turn around, I may fall back to the planet, burn up in the atmosphere. Space is warmer than I thought it would be; Elton John said it was cold as hell, but he's wrong. It's like a heated swimming pool at midnight. And there's not supposed to be any oxygen, but it's no problem breathing. Shouldn't my face and eyeballs swell until they pop out like in *Total Recall?* Space is kind, forgiving, and bigger than anything you've ever thought of.

The moon is the size of a nickel and getting bigger. It's chrome like the trim on a '59 Cadillac. It's brighter out in space than from the earth. Looks like a drop of mercury against the indescribable blackness of nothing.

I can see cracks and bumps in its surface, but it's not the moon at all. It's a whale, a perfect white whale reflecting silver light back to me. A sliver of darkness forms as its mouth opens. It's trying to speak to me.

Time is a motherfucker, Chuck.

Man once thought his future was predetermined by God, what was called predestination. Entire sects of Christianity adhered to this idea. Other religions have destiny and fate, the inevitable futures of each individual. The entire concept of free will was debated.

As man evolved, his concept of the future evolved as well. We have a choice. We can do what we want. We can alter our future with any number of choices, some small, some gargantuan in consequence.

But what of his past? Can't our past be as undetermined as our future? The idea of a solitary past is archaic as Calvinistic predestination ideas.

Your past is like a kite's tail, whipping violently behind your present. You only remember it one way, but your memory is constantly changing, moving with it across different events and times.

Your past is like a dog's tail, and you're fucking with the dog. You're moving the dog, and the tail is moving with it, into pasts you've never had and away from the past you want.

Your past is like a snake's tail, and you're shoving its tail into its mouth. You're making an ouroboros out of your existence.

Your existence is a film, and you're splicing the end to the beginning, making a loop that will never end, an infinite, futile movie.

You're fucking up, Chuck. You have to make this right before you can't undo it. You need to get back to the beginning of your troubles, go back and straighten out your timeline the best you can, and quit fucking with it.

BACK TO THE BUS

I'M WALKING UP to the party-bus rental place. I have to get back to that bus. The party bus. With Eirean and his tech-tard friends. Then I have to smoke out on it. That's the plan.

Something's wrong. Things don't look quite right. I'm still high from something. I can't pin it down, though. I'm really fucked up. I would wait for later, but I feel like I'm being pulled this way. How did I get here? Does it matter?

The receptionist hangs up when she sees me. Then she yells into the intercom.

Ron, we have a crazy homeless guy in here.

I look around, don't see anyone. She's talking about me.

No, I'm not homeless. Well, technically I am, but not in the spirit of the term.

She points mace at me. The guy that must be Ron runs in the room. Ron is a big guy, early fifties, but looks like he's seen some bad days. Like a guy that got huge in prison but has been out for a long time. His hair is white and gray, like Spider-Man's boss. He puts his open palms to me.

Take it easy, guy. Don't do anything dumb.

I want to rent a party bus.

Sure you do. Let's just go outside and talk about it.

Seriously, I have money.

I reach down for my wallet. I realize I'm not wearing a shirt. And I'm dirty, covered in something, I don't know what. The woman yells. Ron freaks out. Woman's on phone again. She's crying and screaming.

Hey hey hey!

Oh, I'm just reaching for my wallet . . .

I pat where the wallet should be. The twenty-five is there instead. Fuck.

Stay cool, bro!

I'm cool. We're all cool. I just need to rent a party bus.

I'm waving the Raven around. I didn't mean to pull it out. Siren. Fuck.

There's some kind of disconnect here, Ron. I know I look bad, but I really need to rent a bus.

Two cops run in. They keep a distance from me, but their Tasers are out. Taser prongs fly at me in slow motion. I hear the other cop talking in sixteen RPM.

We have another one. Covered in fecal matter.

The prongs hit me, bites like a snake. Flash of light. Toes-to-hair pain. Zero G. The floor is the sky, and I'm flying.

Ambulance. Looking at me, two guys, tattoos on their necks, shaved heads. Throat tight. Can't inhale.

Fuck, is he dead, bro?

Not sure. He's on a lot of shit.

He's got a lot of shit on him.

Ha. Yes. Fucking weird.

This is my first shit zombie. Have you seen one of these yet?

Yeah, got one on Sixth Street last week.

You hear we're getting hoses so we can just wash 'em on the spot?

Too little, too late. If the management fucks drove the wagons, they'd fucking have hoses already.

You got that Giants tickets hookup still?

Nah, I broke up with Amanda, and broke up with the hookup in the process.

Fuck. You couldn't wait till the season was over to dump her?

Ha, no. Brutal. Would be lying if I said it didn't cross my mind though. Oh shit.

What?

Check that. Seizure. Don't give him the normal shit though. It's been giving them heart attacks and killing them. Give him a shot of whiteout.

What's in this shit?

No idea. Management says to give 'em this stuff.

In a vein?

No. Do you ever pay attention in meetings? Like an EpiPen. Jam it in his heart. He's more or less OD'ing off whatever he took. Do it. NOW.

Fuck, okay, relax.

He brings what looks like a miniflashlight out, slings it over his head, and jams it into my chest. It's like a pot of boiling water in the face. My stomach swells; my ass fires like a cannon.

Whoa!

Oh god. Oh god.

What the fuck.

Open the back door.

I'm going to fucking hurl. Get an oxygen mask.

He's breathing okay.

For us, shit head, god.

HOSPITAL

WHITE. BRIGHT. FLUORESCENT lights overhead. Like school. Ceiling tiles with tiny holes in a grid pattern.

Pain. All over. Pain. Headache that runs down my spine. Skin numb but pain on inside.

Can't move. Head moves. Arms don't. Legs don't.

Mouth filled with chalk and cigarette ash.

Fuck. I'm in the hospital. I'm strapped down.

Oh yes. Taser.

Is he awake?

I'm not sure. His eyes are open. Not responding completely. Did his results come back?

Yes. Cocaine, and a lot of other substances we can't identify. Experimental street garbage.

We really need to figure out what these guys are taking.

Fading. Numbness. Dry mouth. Ammonia. Sleep.

Wake. Aching. Constricted.

A blurry man comes into view.

Are you awake? Yes, but no. Still out of it, huh? Tasered, sedated, and coming down off whatever's in your system. Horrible combination. Look on the bright side: this is probably the worst you'll ever feel without being dead. Every day from now on, you'll feel better. Can't talk though? I'll come back later.

He leaves. Who was that? Nurse? Doctor? Cop?

Sinking. Lying in a bed of white mud. Sleep.

●

Moving. Rolling. Bed rolling.

Gut hurts. Feels like Tyson punched me twice. Fucking Taser.

Tongue thick. Open mouth. Air tastes like smoke. Close mouth. Tongue raw, swollen, sore. Teeth sharp.

Must ask where I'm going. Nothing comes out.

Easy there, son, you'll be okay.

Pinprick. Fire. Water. Ice cream. Sleep.

I'm in a cell of some kind. It's a simple room with a toilet and sink. Doesn't look like jail though. Something different.

I'm not strapped down anymore. Stiff. Hurts to move, compelled to not stay still.

Stand. Stumble. Catch myself against the wall. Feel tall.

Scream. Throat dry.

Get a drink from the sink. Cup the water to my hand. Good as drugs when you're this thirsty.

Hey, how you doin?

It's a raggedy voice. Harsh, gargling.

Who are you?

Janitor. We were all worried about you.

I see him, looking through the food slot. Yellow eyes with dark brown orbs in the center. Black guy.

Where am I?

SF General. Psych unit. Suicide watch.

I didn't try to kill myself.

I know. We all know. You was 5150 for sure. Smeared in shit and shirtless. 5150 for sure. Talking crazy that you wanted a party bus. 5150 for sure. Had a water gun on you filled with pee. 5150 for sure.

He laughs like I said something funny. Amuses himself, I guess. Water gun? What the fuck?

Stomach rumbles. Knife in the guts.

Detox is a bitch. The pain I can handle. It's the feeling of every bad piece of news you've ever heard coming to you at once. It's a sadness you soak in. It's lead-lined pajamas. It's a dull, heavy nothing matters. The worst is knowing it all goes away with the push of one button. More drugs, and this stops.

Okay, Death, come for me. I'm ready. From all the bullshit times I cheated you, I'm ready now. I won't fight. Just get me out of this mess and turn me off forever.

I wait. Twenty minutes. An hour? I can't tell the passage of time. Fuck. Bored. I'm here for days, or just a little while. I don't know anymore.

I wish it all would stop. This whole thing. The hustle of all this. It's like one of those Chinese finger trap things. The more I struggle to get out, the more I get stuck. I need to make not even the big score, just a good one and split. I have to get out of here. Start over. Go somewhere where no one knows me, some piece-of-shit small town where you can get by working at the gas station or the video store or whatever, some small town where they still have video stores, I guess.

I used to want to be something, something bigger than regular life. I thought I'd be a famous writer or a screenwriter or something. Not someone huge, you know, just cool. Like a B-list guy. I didn't even dream big. I just dreamed above average. Not a bestselling author but one with a dedicated following. Someone with name recognition.

I would travel to different cities and give readings, and it wouldn't be packed but it would be full. In one of those places, a woman would be there who really understood me through the Rorschach tests that my books were. She'd really be able to see deep into me. Me. The real me.

Fuck. I was at least supposed to be good at something. I'm not. I'm good at taking care of MiniWhales, and there's no job for that anymore.

I was at least supposed to be cool. I think I was for a little while. I was a bit of a guy. A scenester. God help me, I was a fucking hipster, although I never would've admitted that at the time.

I was cool between the ages of about twenty-two and twenty-eight, and then it all slid into the shitslide of middle age, early. I got a job at a cool bar at twenty-two and suddenly I was cool. I got in free to cool shows. I met cool girls. I got to stay after hours at other cool bars. I lived in a cool party flat with cool roommates. Cool places with cool people doing cool things and fucking each other later in cool apartments. That's all being cool is—surrounding yourself with other people and having everyone agree that everything you're doing is fucking cool.

Six years of that shit. Being cool. That bar went out of business, and when I tried to get more work, everything was DJs and shit. No more rock clubs. No more being cool.

Young people didn't want bands anymore; they wanted a jackass with a box of fucking records. Not even good music. I went to an '80s night, thinking it would be the good tracks of punk and new wave and what used to be called college rock and then became alternative rock in the next decade.

Washed up at twenty-eight. Done. I kept trying, though. One bullshit gig after another, and every year I got further away from cool. My thirties? Forget it. I hated what was cool. I stopped going to places other people liked. If it got too popular, fuck it.

My cool friends bailed out. They got married, had ironic weddings, and had kids and named them Damien or Exene, or they went with vintage names like Ezekiel and Malachi. Now every grade school is full of Zacks and no one is named John or Dave anymore and every PTA meeting is full of parents with full sleeve tattoos and retro haircuts. Funny, all those fuckers who played poor until it came time to buy a house, and then they had money from somewhere, they had a kid and bought a Subaru Outback, they bought a house in Bernal or Glen Park and talked about equity and interest rates like they used to talk about record labels.

Some died and some became homeless; others disappeared into the chaos, filling the state prisons and haunting the basements of their relatives' houses. They're the junkies on Capp Street and the dead-eyed bums in the Civic Center. They're the zombies on Jones Street and the creeping undead of San Pablo Avenue. They're annoyances and smells and things in the way of rich people walking down the sidewalk. They made poor neighborhoods interesting, so the wealthy moved in, and now they're the scourge of the same streets. They're John and Jane Does that are found in ditches and pulled out of lakes. They're the donated cadavers for medical students, cremated by the state, and the only club they'll ever be in is the potter's field.

They're gone now, they're all dead to me as far as I'm concerned, and I'm dead to them. Maybe I'm a picture in a scrapbook no one looks at anymore, or a part of a group-therapy story someone tells and they can't remember my name. I'm a guy they got a tattoo with, the guy who let them into the show when it was sold out, that one roommate that only lived here a month, what was his name?

For a while, it seemed like everyone knew me and I knew everyone who mattered. Now I know a couple of people here and there, enough to get by, but no one really close to me. I'm stuck in here and no one is going to miss me—someday someone might ask, *Whatever happened to that guy?* and they'll look it up on the computer or phone app or whatever people are using to keep up with those they don't care about, and they won't find out anything.

Now here I am in the psych ward at SF General on suicide watch or some shit. Fuck this. Really. How did I get from there to here? I'm technically homeless now. I'm a homeless drug addict who was covered in shit and is now in the Nutty Buddy.

I'm in the day room watching *Seinfeld*. It's the one where George eats an éclair out of the trash. The walls are the color of a nicotine stain. It smells like Mountain Dew and Pine-Sol in here. Sweet, artificial, over the faint odor of microwave-heated marinara sauce.

They're calling a name over and over on the intercom. I can't hear the show. Dallas Luxury, a transgender nightclub singer, taps me on the shoulder.

Sweetie, she says, *they're calling your name.*

She has a bruise running from the middle of her forearm all the way past the elbow. She fought the cops, and the cops won. She gotten 86'd from a bar and had refused to leave. The cops were called, and she put up a fight. She got slammed to the sidewalk and the full MMA treatment from some meathead cops. She's a pain in the ass, but it's totally unnecessary to hurt someone like that.

I make my way to the front desk.

I pass Larry, who smells like he's been hotboxing cigarettes, although he never has any and we wouldn't be allowed to smoke them even if we were allowed to have them. He has a stash somewhere and a smoke spot. I have to find out where it is.

There's a guy at the front desk waiting for me. He's in a suit and is either a detective or works for the AVN Awards. Has a mustache like a drive-through car wash.

He's saying something, but I can't really understand what it is. Catching one out of every four or five words. Too fast or too loud or something. Fuck, it must be the meds.

He's going to get me out of here. Like now. He signs a paper and asks me something. He repeats it. I finally get it.

Do you have any personal items?

No. No. Nothing. I don't have anything.

Let's go.

I follow him to the elevator. The door opens. We get in.

You doing okay, Chuck?

I guess. Feel a little dopey.

I bet.

We ride the rest of the way to the ground floor. I still feel like it's some kind of trick. He's whistling something I don't recognize; it's shrill to my sensitive ears.

The doors open, and the light of the sky hits me. Fuck, it's bright. Psych ward is dim—fluorescent lights, and half of them are out, maybe more. It's a dark place, full of corners and shadows and doubts. I squint, shield my eyes, but there's not really sun out, it's just glowing clouds. Still, a little hotter than I'd like it.

The air is amazing after being locked up in the psych ward for . . . how long was I in there? That place smelled like cleaning products and farts. Institutional food farts. The worst kind. No matter what you have to eat, it always smells like onion soup powder.

He drives a Chrysler 300. Not cop issue. Who is this guy? I hesitate.

GET. IN.

I get in. There's a sack on the seat. I feel warm.

There's a change of clothes in there. Plus your wallet, your phone, and your twenty-five. Oh yeah, your gun. I had the report changed to read you had a water pistol full of urine. Keeps with the whole "I'm covered in shit" motif you were rocking. No one gives a shit about your little popgun. You can keep that. You might need it.

Who are you?

I told you already. Agent Hart from the FBI. You've been remanded to my custody.

What do you mean, I might need this?

You do know about Liza, right? They told you? Hell, they thought it was why you had your psychotic break.

What? Liza? What happened . . . tell me.

They found her cut up.

Stabbed?

No. Cut into pieces. With only a few strokes. Just like your old boss, Eirean. That's why I'm here. It looks like it may be a serial killer. Sorry to tell you. Do you know anyone who would want to hurt both her and Eirean?

No.

It's likely someone you know. The chances of both of these being random and you knowing both without knowing the killer are slim to none.

I have no idea.

The murder weapon is what is strange. It has characteristics of a knife wound and an axe wound, while not looking like either. Do you know anyone who collects medieval weapons?

Vietnam John. That fucker. He killed them with that crazy knife. Why? It's hot, but the window won't roll down.

There's another matter.

He reaches in his breast pocket and pulls out a marble.

Tell me what you know about this.

It's a marble?

No, it's much more than that. No time to bullshit me. I don't care about you being locked up.

Can you turn on the air conditioner?

You okay? You're not going to boot in here, are you? You want me to pull over?

Where are we going?

FBI safe house. You'll like it.

Nah, just drop me off somewhere . . .

Where? Where are you going to go? You think I don't know what I'm doing? You're homeless. There's nowhere to drop you off.

What do you care?

I need to be able to find you again. It's hard to find people that don't have a place to live. Plus, I have your meds.

Meds?

Yep. You're on some crazy shit. I don't even know if this is FDA approved yet.

What is it?

I don't know the medical term, but everyone's calling it whiteout. It's the latest thing they're coming up with to counteract this black hole shit that you fuckers are all smoking until you go crazy and smear yourselves with shit.

All what?

All you fuckers. There's one or two a day in the Bay Area now. The DEA is trying to keep it contained, but it's only a matter of time. If this spreads out to the rest of the US, we're in deep shit, no pun intended.

He keeps talking. Sounds like real conspiracy shit. They know everything, but everything they know is wrong. A bunch of people who don't smoke it who think they can get in our heads. They can't. They have to smoke it. They have to be one of us. But of course, they're no longer them at that point.

All through South Beach, shit has changed. Used to be warehouses; there was even a weird trailer park down here on Townsend Street back in the day. Now it's all luxury condos and upscale restaurants. All people do here is work at tech jobs, sleep in million-dollar condos, and eat for entertainment. I guess they drink, too. There are bars that pop up down here that serve nothing but top-shelf mojitos and appletinis or whatever the trendy drink is at the time.

Agent Hart's place is all glass and views above the Bay. Everything is new. Everything is nice. Everything looks like it fits together. It's so clean, I can immediately smell myself.

Take a shower, he says, pointing in the direction. *You smell like the psych ward.*

I'm so used to tiny flats stuffed with roommates in every corner, under the stairs, in the pantry, in bunk beds, with old plumbing that hasn't been replaced in forty years that I have no idea how most of the city is living.

The shower is clean. It doesn't drip. When I turn the hot faucet, hot water comes out. I bet I could flush in here and it wouldn't change a damn thing. I scrub as much as I can, trying to get the institutional stink off me.

The meds are like eating a hot pepper, if your entire body was your mouth. They're keeping me rooted in time. I'm clean, more or less, for the first time since . . . seventeen? I take the meds when I'm naked and standing in the shower. Once they hit, I feel like Johnny Storm flaming on. I sweat immediately and my heart punches through my chest. But I don't have withdrawals.

Agent Hart isn't a bad guy. He's like the class president in high school. Popular but not an asshole, but nothing interesting about him, either. The guy who gets A's and plays three sports. The guy whose hair is always in place, drives a cool car that was handed down to him, and has a girlfriend who always says hi and smiles at you but will never really talk to you. The couple you picture having functional sex for the first time on prom night and mutually climaxing.

He watches *CSI* and *Law & Order* and a few other cop shows I don't recognize. We watch *Casino* and *Goodfellas*, *Scarface*, *Menace II Society*, *Road House*, and *The Big Lebowski*. His favorite movie is *The Shawshank Redemption*. This guy is the living average guy in his age group. He's a demographic. He's a walking pie chart off the Life page of the *USA Today*. How do you get like this? How do you get to be an average guy with an above-average job and do everything you're supposed to do, like contribute to your 401(k) and shit like that?

He eats everything but in moderation. He has a beer sometimes and drinks a bit of scotch but that's it. I tried sneaking some of his scotch, but it's not working with the meds I'm on. Makes me instantly nauseous.

This is the best place I've ever lived. It has everything I need. But it's weird, not going outside. It's a prison cell with a premium cable package and a fully stocked fridge, a Tempur-Pedic mattress and a showerhead with multiple settings. I'm restless. I want to go outside. I think of bolting out of here. But I also know I'll never live this well again.

Time for us to go, he says, turning off the TV.

Go? Go where?

You've gone through sufficient detox. I can take you outside out in the real world.

What for?

I need you to spot for me. You see a world out there that I only know exists in theory. I'm looking for what I think is there, and not only do you know what it looks like, you also have a name for it.

What are you looking for?

The killer with the axe or the halberd or whatever it is. A broadsword. Also, the black hole source is somewhere in the Tenderloin, from looking at the occurrence of . . .

Shit zombies?

For lack of a better word.

No. This is death. I just want to go into witness relocation or something.

That's for witnesses in federal cases. You're not in one of those yet. Yet. We make a case, and I can assuredly get you set up in a new place with a new name.

A sweet pad like this?

Yeah. You should see what we have in Miami.

Fuck Miami. Fuck Florida.

Okay then. We'll set you up in a state of your choice. But we have to get a case going first before we make you a witness that we have to protect.

No. No, it's death. For sure. These guys are bad news.

What about Liza?

What about her?

You loved her. Right?

It wasn't really love, per se.

Fine, whatever. But you were in each other's lives and she cared about you, and some asshole chopped her into lunchmeat. Don't you want to see justice done?

Liza. Hell. She was nice to me. She swiped a bunch of my drugs, but I probably would've done the same in her situation. Fuck.

This is one last hustle. Do this, this last bit of dirt, and then retire wherever. Alaska. I could go to Alaska. Live off the grid in some cabin getting a check from the government. I could get a seaplane or some shit. Solar panels and Netflix and I'm good. Or Montana. Raise llamas.

Fuck, everyone snitches. Everyone rolls eventually. That whole thing of never ratting out is fiction. It's only in movies. It's not real. Everyone gets caught doing something dumb like shooting dope and nodding out in the getaway car or their girlfriend gets mad and calls the cops and drops dime. It's my turn.

I don't owe these fuckers anything. I'm just a means to an end. I'm an ATM you put drugs in and money comes out. Well, no more, jack—this ATM is offline.

I'll do it, I say, standing up quickly.

That's my boy, he says, holding out a fist to bump.

OSO'S PLACE

I HAVEN'T BEEN out of the TL that long, but it looks worse than I remember. It's a shade dirtier, a little bit smellier; there's a few more broken windows, a couple more graffiti tags; the sidewalks have an extra junkie or two hanging out. It just looks like it has upped its filth game one level. Like an extra layer of grime coating the place.

We pull up outside Oso's place. The plan is this: I get in there and confirm Oso is in there with a bunch of shit. I drop a code word into the mike, and a van full of testosterone and Kevlar empties out and storms the castle. A small group of trigger-happy motherfuckers that want to make a video-game-style mess out of anyone who gets in their way, to turn their problem into a fine red mist.

Agent Hart adjusts a microphone made to look like an Eat the Rich button.

You have your gun?

Yes.

Is it loaded? One in the chamber?

Yes, Mom.

You wouldn't think of skipping on me with that buy money, would you?

The only thing I would do with a stack of money like this is buy drugs. And that's what I'm supposed to do with it.

I get out of the car. Something's not right down here. It's hard to say that the air in the TL is bad, but it's like the air is stained or something, a dingy yellow color all around me. Not smoke, but something like it. It's like the air isn't clear, like it has a slight tinge to it.

The buzzer on Oso's building is like something you'd find on a gas station bathroom floor. It's so dirty there is hair and grit stuck to it. I don't want to touch it, but I have to press the buttons with something. Pocket check. Wallet. Gun. That's it.

Fuck. This is what my life has come to? I'm a guy who only carries a wallet and a pistol? I should at least have a pen. I could go back to the car and get one, I guess. No, fuck that. I buzz up with my pinky. Must remember not to touch the eyes or mouth with this pinky.

The front hallway already stinks to high hell. I'm not even on Oso's floor, and I can smell him. Flies sit on the banister like birds on a wire. They don't fly away as my hand goes up the rail. I have to avoid them. Some of them walk slowly, but they don't fly.

The smell is so overwhelming when I get to his door that I want to bolt out of here. I want to tell Hart that it didn't work out, that he wasn't there. I close my eyes, think of my cabin in Alaska, and knock.

It's open, fool, I hear him say. I turn the knob. A rush of warm, spoiled air and a squadron of flies escape into my face. I exhale and try to inhale, and it's worse the second time. I see those little floaty things in front of my eyes.

You okay, fool?

Yeah, just a little sick. I need to get right.

You got my money, motherfucker?

Wouldn't come back around without it.

My eyes quit stinging and adjust.

Oso isn't fat.

What. The. Fuck.

Oso isn't fat, but he has long, sagging wrinkles. He's wearing a bathrobe. It's open, but with the overlapping folds of skin, I can't see his cock, only drooping flesh trying to ooze its way to the floor. His skin has tiny lumps all over it.

Heard you got picked up on a 5150.

Yeah.

I can't front you no more.

Not asking you to.

Oso's moving slowly, like he's underwater. He's trying to stand up, I think. His whole body shines with sweat. He gets in a standing position and drips rings on his carpet.

Hey, bro . . . do you smell something weird?

You're kidding, right?

Oso falls to the floor. Dark chili vomit shoots out of his mouth. Thousands of black hole marbles surface from his skin. They were waiting to break out of him like that urban legend of the lady who had a spider lay eggs in her ear.

There's millions of dollars of black hole marbles all over the place emerging from the corpse of the worst smelling man I've ever met. I'm alternating between greed, shock, and disgust.

The vomit smell hits me, and while I thought this room couldn't get any worse, I immediately puke everything I have and dry heave. I have to get out of here. But I can't pass up the bounty in this room.

This apartment is full of money and drugs, the two solutions to all my problems.

Fuck all this. Fuck it all. Fuck the feds and whatever plans they have. Now that Oso is dead, I don't even know what they want from me. They don't need me. Fuck. I should get what I can and bail on this whole scene.

They must be on their way. I have to hurry.

I scoop up what I can of the black hole marbles and put them in my pockets. They're too heavy. I need something to put them in. I dump them back out on the floor.

I try to open the windows, but they're stuck. Dry heaving. Should I break one? Would that draw too much attention? Fuck it. It's the TL. No one cares about a fucking broken window.

I break one with the butt of my twenty-five. Blood. Fuck. Cold wind comes in. Bleeding everywhere. Hand or arm or finger or something is bleeding. It's getting all over.

Cookie tin in the kitchen. I can dump the cookies out and put the marbles in it. I open the tin. Cocaine. A cookie tin full of cocaine. I scoop up a huge bump with a delivery menu lying on the counter. Oh fuck. This shit is clean. Uncut. There's not coke like this around anymore. Heart Panics. Going to burst. I'm sexy. I'm a god. I took too much. FUCK THE WORLD.

Keep looking. Always something under the sink.

Money. Stacks of it, wrapped in plastic. Stuff stack of hundreds in the pants. That's coming with me.

I can hear them climbing the fire escape. They're coming in. Fuck. Must leave, now.

Run down the hall. Old lady getting in the elevator. Get on.

She's covered in cat hair, and I'm covered in blood and puke. She doesn't pay me any mind. Stops. Run out.

Outside.

Agent Hart stands outside the car. He's looking at me. He knows something's wrong.

Behind him is Vietnam John with the biggest knife I've ever seen.

Vietnam John. Behind you. BEHIND YOU.

Slow motion. Silence. Hart sees my fear and turns around. Vietnam John has the knife overhead. Hart reflexively puts his forearm above his face.

Hart's arm severs right above the elbow and flies off like it's waving goodbye. The stump shoots a foot-long arc of blood across John's face. Hart drops. John's knife is stuck in the car. It's split part of the roof and gotten wedged in.

John looks up at me. Our eyes lock. Rage stare.

You're part of this, you son of a bitch! he yells. *Snitch rat motherfucker!*

There's no time to explain. Run. Fucking run. Don't look back, just run. There's a bookstore on Market. I know where the employee bathroom is. Hide.

HIDEY HOLE

I DON'T THINK anyone saw me come in here.

Calm down. Relax. Breathe. Take inventory.

Hart had my meds. My replacement meds they put me on at the hospital. I'm not even sure what it was.

I can't get back into his place.

There will be a swarm of cops around his car.

I'm probably a suspect in some part of this.

Ten grand in cash.

I feel around in my pockets. One solitary black hole marble. When I dumped them out, I must have missed this one.

There's a faint smell in here of weed. Stale, old weed.

I look behind a bookshelf. A pipe and a lighter. Not the best, but it will do.

When in doubt, get high. If you don't know what you're doing, do it blasted out of your mind. You can always blame the drugs for any bad decisions you make. It's a lot easier than having to blame yourself. If you can't fix what's broken, break it some more.

Being strung out beats withdrawals by a long shot. I'm not facing all this bullshit without being high. That's for damn sure. I'm not going back to SF General. Fuck that place. If there's no real way of getting this shit out of my system, I'm going the other direction. I'm putting a lot more in my system.

There's nothing like your first high, but a high after a detox and a long clean spell, well, that's probably second.

I hit the marble with the lighter. It takes a moment, but a trail of smoke wisps off it, and I inhale and hold it. I haven't exhaled, and I can feel it getting into my system. This bathroom is my world, and I am a king. Yertle the Turtle of this sixteen-square-foot pond. Everything is perfect.

My heart is pounding. I can hear it like it's outside my chest. Wait, it's not my heart.

Someone's banging on the door.

Sir? Sir? This bathroom is for employees only.

I work here.

No, you don't.

Yes, I do. I just started.

I saw you go in. You don't work here. You need to leave, or we're calling the police.

Call 'em. I can't hurry this up. I'm in pain.

You're getting high. I can smell it.

What do you smell?

Marijuana and something else like burnt plastic. Crack? Meth?

You're getting warmer.

Seriously, asshole.

Yes. I'm totally serious. Five minutes, and I swear, I will leave and never come back.

Smoke me out?

Really?

Yeah. This job sucks. Smoke me out and we're cool.

Done.

I let the kid in.

He's late teens or maybe twenty. His hair looks like he spent a long time getting it to look shitty.

Okay, hurry, pass it.

You don't want to know what it is?

I, sir, give not one fuck. I hate this job. If it gets me through the day here, all the better.

Here. It's called black hole.

Sick.

The kid tries to fire it a couple of times and inhale, and nothing happens. Then he fires it and holds it until it starts smoking. This kid's been high before. I see the change happen in his face.

Oh fuck. This is good.

Yeah, it does the job.

You mind if I hit it a little more?

All you want.

The kid takes a huge hit and holds it until I think he's going to pass out. His eyes are closed. He opens them for a bit and he's totally yakked.

There's a weird guilt about turning someone on to a drug you know will probably fuck them up. But you know, every time someone got me high for free, I really appreciated it. If you're giving someone drugs who wouldn't normally need or take them, that's one thing, but for someone like me, the only thing standing between me and not getting high was not having drugs. Someone not sharing with me was only delaying something that would happen anyway.

He exhales. Laughs.

This shit is AMAZING.

It is, isn't it?

We should get out of here. My manager told me to run you out.

I open the door.

The store looks different.

I turn around. The kid is gone. The books on the shelf are different.

I walk out. There's a stack of newspapers by the front door.

It's 1988.

There's nowhere better to hide than the past. Vietnam John will never find me here. The feds will never find me. None of that shit has happened yet.

I have ten grand in cash in 1988, and that's like twenty or thirty now, or will be. Or however this works.

Fuck. The new hundreds. Those goofy big-headed Franklins don't exist yet.

I duck back in the bathroom. Sort out the bills. Out of the hundred hundred-dollar bills, ten of them are old enough to use. That's more money than I ever had then. I'll be fine.

1988. What to do now?

Where am I? I think I'm in LA right now, planning a move to SF. Should I try to warn myself of all this? Should I convince myself to get my shit together and go to a good school and learn computers?

That wouldn't work. I wouldn't listen.

So what should I do?

If you don't know what to do in 1988, you look at flyers. There's no Internet, no social media, and no apps to check. Phones are still attached to poles and walls. TV sucks.

I look at a wall of an empty storefront. It's covered with layer upon layer of flyers. And finally, I see what I'm looking for. A punk show at a warehouse in the Mission. Who else but Op Ivy?

I'm by far the oldest guy at this show. They probably think I'm some creep or maybe someone's dad. This band is as good as everyone said it was. Out in the parking lot, a younger me is passed out in a van.

I could try to warn myself, but young me is way too fucked up right now, and even if I did get me awake, I would never believe this bullshit.

In true East Bay punk fashion, Op Ivy broke up way too early, and they became legends having never played in their prime; all their shows were their early days, if you think about it one way. The amount of people who claim to have seen them is about four or five times as many as people who actually saw them.

There's probably a dozen or so people I know in here right now, right before I will meet them in a few months to a year. These are their teenage selves.

I walk through the crowds, looking into faces. The skin is young and unscarred for the most part. These are teens who feel like old people—god, I felt like I had seen it all; I felt washed up and done at nineteen. I looked like all of these kids. There was so much future, but it felt like the world was ending at dawn.

When I started listening to punk, Black Flag and the Dead Kennedys had already broken up, other bands like Minor Threat were long gone, and the bands like the Ramones were playing huge venues and already seemed like a nostalgia act. I thought I had missed everything.

Everything I was into—music, film, poetry—had just passed its heyday if you asked anyone who was involved. The story was that everything was better and cheaper five years ago and now it sucks and its all been ruined by posers or yuppies or Christians or some shit.

Of course, things were great, and there was a lot of great shit around, but it's hard to notice when you're there. When it's in front of you, you don't realize how special it is, how much it will mean to you. It's all the other things—the shows were better because of the friends you went with, the getting there and back, when it wasn't easy to get to a show, cramming six into a car that seats four and getting all of you in for fifteen dollars when it should cost eighteen.

I think I see Liza at the front of the stage. God, she's so cute. She's like seventeen or something. She would've made my teenage brain explode. She has that Chelsea fringe that was popular with the skinhead and mod girls at the time. It's bleached bright—must've done it right before the show. The little skull tattoos right below her neck are new. She got those on the run from teenage rehab. Later, she'll get them covered with roses. I want to say hi to her, but I can't. How would I explain any of that? Just enjoy the band.

More often than not, how you remember things is not how they happened. You remember how you felt while they were happening. You remember your emotions. But what was happening is not what caused those emotions. Being with your friends made you feel good, and the band, in reality, sucked ass, but you didn't care because you had a crew full of guys you cared about, they had your back, and you had theirs.

Now that you're old enough to get to a show without a problem, you've forgotten what that's like; you drive your Prius to a punk show and pay to park. You watch the show and someone tells you the guitarist was from another band, the drummer is nineteen, and well, this isn't really the band anymore, is it? The singer is the same, and he's playing all the hits, and the sold-out crowd at The Warfield gives up a cheer as each song starts as if to tell everyone, *I like this song, this is my favorite, I'm a real fan.* But it's only slightly better than a karaoke band; it's a wedding band for rich aging punks. What happened? The songs are the same, but you've changed. You went to a show by yourself because you lost touch with your old friends or they moved away or they won't go out on a night when they work the next day. Instead of enjoying the band's songs, you spend the whole show worried about whether or not someone's breaking into your car.

Op Ivy finishes up. I wish I could just rewind all this and watch it again. There's a drug for that, or there will be in the future, and I'd love to have it right now.

Hotel room on Sixteenth smells like an old sock. Ears are ringing from the show. Haven't eaten in . . . since the '80s started, I guess. Exhausted but won't be able to sleep real sleep.

That half sleep of the strung out and coming down. It's like you're staring at the insides of your eyelids. It's a Rothko painting. It's the void. It's a red that any darker would be black, but red enough that you can't sleep. Not really. Sometimes your body shuts down, it has sleep paralysis; sometimes you can hear yourself snore, but you're stuck there, for hours, with your body passed out and your mind wide awake in freakout mode.

It's the boredom that makes me crazy. The pure boredom. Alone with my thoughts, there's nothing worse for me. I need stimulation. TV. Talk radio. Books. Podcasts. Movies. I don't care. I need to hear things, other thoughts than my own. My own thoughts while coming down are like a pop song played repeatedly.

I could smoke more. Get high. But who knows where I'd end

up. When I'd end up. If I don't smoke again, I can stay here. Move to Reno or Vegas or something and make millions betting on sports. I should buy some Starbucks stock. Fuck. Microsoft, Apple. I could build a crazy portfolio. Just don't smoke anything.

But I'm itchy. I'm itchy and stiff. Nothing's comfortable.

Fuck, I need a drink.

Walk across the street. Cars honking, headlights trail off. Feet hurt. I should get new shoes.

Liquor store. Bright lights, tinnitus hum. Fluorescents flickering in a pattern. Round mirror in the corner. I look like shit. I look like a crackhead, and there's plenty out right now. Luckily, no one gives a shit about another crackhead on San Pablo.

Six pack of cokes. Bag of ice.

Fifth of Jim Beam, please.

Do you have money?

What? Yes, I have fucking money.

I take out a twenty and throw it on the counter. He puts all the stuff in a thin plastic bag.

There's a junkie wearing Saran Wrap underneath his shirt. He's like a clear plastic mummy under his clothes. I can see it sticking out. I don't know why, and I don't want to know. It's more drug-addict bullshit. He has a hood pulled down over his face. Creepy as fuck.

Bag strains, stretches out with the weight of the cans and ice. Don't let it tear open. Hold it like a baby.

Saran Wrap wants to talk to me. I can feel it.

Hey. Hey man, let me talk to you for a minute.

Ignore him. Keep walking. Don't engage.

Hey. Hold up.

Fuck this guy. He wants what's in my bag, and he has nothing I want.

Hey, I just want to talk to you.

Switch tactics: *Fuck you.*

Hey, don't be like that.

I don't want to talk with you. Beat it.

I know you.

No, you don't.

I know you, from the future. Chuck. Right? That's it, right?

Stops me. Chills. Fuck. I do know that voice. Andy. NSA Andy.

Please, I just want to talk to you.

Okay, yes, follow me. Hurry.

Shoes feel like lumpy steel. Joints ache. Headlights trail off. Doppler honking.

Hotel room. TV on. *WKRP* rerun. I make Beam and Coke cocktails in plastic cups. Take a long drink. Doesn't feel like much, but it's refreshing going down. I hand one to Andy.

I swear to god, I thought turkeys could fly.

What? Andy says, taking his drink.

It's the last line of this episode.

Did you get sucked here through the black hole, too?

Yeah.

How do we get back?

I don't know if we do. Well, I don't know how to get back to the right place. But if we smoke up again, we'll be somewhere else.

Let's do it. Do you have yours still? I lost mine.

No. I'm good here. The '80s were better. Easier to navigate. I go back, and it's all bullshit. And I've seen what happens to you.

What?

Sorry. No. I shouldn't tell you. Maybe it still won't happen.

I flip around on TV. It's the World Series game with the Dodgers and the A's. Gibson is up.

Oh, I love this game, I say, *It's a classic.*

Baseball is corporate bullshit.

You're in my hotel room, Andy, drinking my liquor. Shut up, drink, and watch. I just want to get drunk and see if it takes the edge off these withdrawals.

Baseball is a tool of the government.

Shut up, Andy. Drink. Watch.

Hoping this shit hits my system. It burns in my throat and cools it right after. Hell yes.

Gibson strikes out.

That's not what happens.

What?

This game . . . this game is a famous game. Gibson comes up to bat and wins the game with a home run.

That's not what happened this time.

That's exactly my fucking point. Gibson gets the home run.

That's not set in stone. In every universe in which this guy . . . what's his name?

Gibson. Kirk Gibson.

In every universe in which this precise moment happens, he has a chance to either hit it or get an out, right?

No. I've seen this happen.

Listen to me. You saw this guy at this moment once before. Right?

Yes.

Every time, in every universe in which this precise moment happens, it plays out any number of ways: a base hit, a home run, a strikeout, whatever. You've seen it be a home run. This time, it's a strikeout. It wasn't some kind of pure destiny that Kirk Gibson hits this home run. What are the chances of him hitting one?

Slim to none. He was hurt; he could barely walk.

And that's what makes it a great moment. You saw something that probably exists in less than 1 percent of the universes in which this moment exists.

You're hurting my brain.

No, I'm helping you. Listen. No matter what the humans do on this earth, the earth still spins. That's what matters to the space-time continuum. Not whether your parents meet or not, not this home run, not any of the fucking wars or anything you think really matters on earth. Not even if humans ever evolved. The earth forms, and there's this tiny chance over billions of years that humans end up happening, so if you think that some poem you write or some baby you make matters one way or another to the way the planet spins, you're fucking out of your god damned mind. The planet doesn't give a shit whether or not you're on it. Neither does the solar system, the galaxy, or anything else in fucking space. Got it?

No, someone else tried to explain this to me another time, and I feel a lot like I do now.

Trust me. This is how the shit is.

So the Oakland A's take game one of the '88 World Series. Fuck. Maybe they still take game two. That would put them at two up rather than tied. Then the Dodgers win the next two, but instead of that winning the whole thing, they just tie up the series. Maybe the A's take it.

Sure. Whatever. Let me ask you this: does any of it matter? Really?

Yes. What happens matters.

Yes, what happens in each universe does matter, to that universe only. Things have a way of evening out. Picture pouring water through a pipe. Each time you pour it through, the molecules have an infinite amount of ways to interact and get through the pipe, but at the end of the day, all you care about is did the water get through the pipe or not? Imagine each water molecule was sentient and wrote thesis statements and opened small businesses and got on Star Search—they would all be thinking they're important when, in fact, they don't matter to you, me, or the pipe one fucking bit. You take the same water and pass it through the pipe again. It all comes out, but infinitely different each time.

I still don't get how this has to do with me.

The black hole puts us at different points in the time pipe. We're the water, and we're pouring through the time pipe over and over again.

Your mind is pouring through a crack pipe. You're fucking nuts.

I'm the only sane one left.

Just you wait. I'll be getting high with strippers while you're smeared in shit and running down the street.

Now who's crazy?

Let's just watch TV and drink.

I wake up. Something's gripping my spine. Fuck this hurts. I move, it calms, then hurts. I move and it calms again.

The lights come on. Interrogation lights. Floodlights. Where am I?

Black hole smoke gets in my nose. I inhale. Hold it.

Easy, bro, you'll be okay.

Andy's blowing smoke into my face. Good god, these are just withdrawals. The pain subsides. My fists unclench. Yes. It's good. Drugs are good.

I snatch the pipe from him and hit it like I stole it.

I hold my breath and wait for it to hit my brain.

The world is a good place. It's full of love, and I am a vessel for its energy. Energy and matter. That's all we are, and we think we're special and unique, but from the point of view of the universe, we're all just slow energy that fucks and eats and kills. Hell yeah.

I open my eyes. Andy is gone.

Someone's banging on the door. They're yelling something.

Fuck it.

Smoke more.

Where the fuck am I?

Blackness. Cold metal. I stand and hit my head. Dumpster.

I lift the lid and stand up. German and Japanese tourists take pictures like it's their last day ever to take pictures.

Scream. They scream and run.

I get out. Sore as fuck. Wander around the side of the building.

I check my teeth. They're all there. I could swear I lost them all.

I'm at the party-bus rental place. If I can find this bus and get high on it, maybe I can get back in the timestream before everything goes to shit and everyone dies. Maybe I can save Liza.

I did this before. I remember this.

I pat my pockets. Gun. Twenty-five. Yes. I storm in.

The receptionist hangs up when she sees me. Then she yells into the intercom.

Ron, we have a crazy homeless guy in here.

She's talking about me.

No, I'm not homeless. Well, technically I am, but not in the spirit of the term.

She points mace at me. The guy that must be Ron runs in the room. Ron is a big guy, early fifties, but looks like he's seen some bad days. Like a guy that got huge in prison but has been out for a long time. His hair is white and gray, like Spider-Man's boss. He puts his open palms to me.

I pull the gun out and make it as menacing as the small pistol can be.

Take it easy, guy. Don't do anything dumb.

I want to rent a party bus.

Sure you do. Let's just go outside and talk about it.

Seriously, just give me the bus, and I'm out. I just need it for an hour or so. Give me the keys to a bus, and no one gets hurt.

The woman yells. Ron freaks out. Woman's on phone again. She's crying and screaming.

Put the fucking phone down and get me some bus keys!

Easy, fella.

The woman puts the phone down and explodes into tears.

I'M GOD DAMNED SERIOUS. I NEED A BUS. I WILL BRING IT THE FUCK BACK. I JUST NEED IT FOR LIKE, A HALF HOUR. FOR FUCK'S SAKE.

Two cops run in. They keep a distance from me, but their Tasers are out. A Taser fires. Two prongs fly at me in slow motion. I hear the other cop talking in sixteen RPM.

We have another one. Covered in fecal matter.

The prongs hit me, bites like a snake. Flash of light. Toes-to-hair pain. Zero G. The floor is the sky, and I'm flying.

Psych ward again.

Wearing the kinder, gentler version of a straitjacket: Velcro straps.

There's a light that stays on above my head. I can close my eyes, but it's never quite dark. I swear I can feel the heat coming off it. The walls pulsate. It's the drugs. They're good, whatever they are.

A sweet-looking old Filipino lady comes in and talks to me. I try to say something back, but I can't. Just drool at her. I can't understand what she's saying. I can't tell if it's English or Tagalog. She's nice, and she cares, and she's bringing me more drugs. That's true love right there.

Next to my bed is an IV drip. She shoots something into that little valve, and I'm immediately floating on a slab of Jell-O. This is some good shit.

I want a TV. I want to listen to something. I'm fucking bored in here. Something. Anything but my own head. This is a god damned waste of good drugs. Put on talk radio, for fuck's sake. Anything that connects me to the outside world, anything to wrap my drug-soaked brain around. Instead I'm listening to the sound of traffic on Potrero, the occasional motorcycle and the bullhorn squawks of the highway patrol.

And the smell . . . the psych ward always smells like someone threw up and someone else tried to clean it but couldn't get it all out. So it smells like microwaved marinara sauce and bleach. Not the smell I want when I'm high.

Our Lady of Drugs leaves the room, and the door shuts.

I wait. Killing time, trying to keep sanity by writing a screenplay in my head. I'll write this whole thing out when I get out of here—now that will be a story. But I'm too fucking high to remember much of what I thought of only a few minutes before.

●

The light blinks out. I wait for someone to come in, but no one does. It must be the middle of the night. Finally, darkness. Maybe the power went out or the bulb burned out. I don't care. I can fully relax for the first time since I got here.

I'm sinking in the blackness, slowly deeper. I see little bubbles coming out of my nose, but I have no trouble breathing. This midnight sky water is cool and refreshing.

A white whale swims toward me. As he approaches, I realize he's not far away, he's small. A MiniWhale. One of mine. I recognize him. The asshole whale. Yes, he's here with me. Someone dumped him in the bay, and he's swum over to me.

He's about a foot from my face. I don't know what his plans are. I want to swim away, but I'm paralyzed. I imagine him biting my face. Clamping on to my temples and cracking my skull like a pecan.

You fucked up this time, Chuck, he says.

Oh yes, I'm high as fuck. I'm not really in the water, and the whale's not really here. So of course he can talk.

You fucked up big time. You fucked up all your last chances. There's no coming back from this one. You're stuck in this space-time bumper car, and you're not getting off.

All you had to do was not get high. Not get loaded. You got sucked in this black hole of your own doing. You were fucking clean. For the first time in your life, you were clean. All you had to do was not do something. You're great at not doing stuff. You're not doing anything RIGHT NOW.

But no. You can't build something up without just knocking it down as soon as possible.

Can you get me out of here, little Moby Dick whale? Can you lead me to the exit? Can I escape with you? Can I swim to the surface and wake up in someone else's body?

The whale swims away, a white jewel shrinking on black velvet.

Someone's in the room with me. I can't move. I can't speak.

Chuck? Are you awake? We have to get out of here. The power went out. There's a crazy man with a giant knife tearing the shit out of this place.

The voice. It belongs to Dallas, the transgender nightclub singer. Hands on me. Sounds of loosening straps and disassembling the IV.

Hold on, honey, we'll get you out of here.

Screams. Sirens. Metal crashing on the floor. Glass breaking.

Someone's moving me. Lifting me up. Setting me down on gurney.

Rolling out of here. Backup emergency lights.

I'm in the back of a car across laps. Dallas yelling at the driver. Cab? Cab. Cab. Where are we going?

Drive, Dallas yells. *Drive, god damn it. FUCKING DRIVE.*

We go. Cop cars all around, racing to SF General.

THE APARTMENT

I WAKE UP. Every muscle is stiff. Everything hurts. Headache like none other.

There are mirrored tiles all over the walls. Lime green ceiling. I move, and the bed moves with me. Fucking waterbed.

I roll myself out. Where the fuck am I?

Naked.

There's a robe on the back of the door. I put it on.

I leave the room and walk to a crowd noise. The living room is full of people from the psych ward. They're drinking mimosas and smoking weed. There are giant framed posters of musicals covering every inch of wall space.

Dallas is holding court, telling some story we've probably all heard.

Zac, the guy who falls in love with strippers. Steffan, who never sleeps. Kristee, the compulsive shoplifter. Miles, sad, sad Miles. They're unshaven with horrible haircuts, their skin a grayish pale. But they're wearing costumes and outlandish clothing.

Chuck! You're awake! Come have a seat. And a drink. And a smoke.

Where are we?

Harris Winchell's place.

The songwriter?

The one. Isn't this place fabulous? He's lived here for forty years. He pays, like, two hundred dollars a month for this place.

Miles hands me a mimosa. I drink it, and it doesn't feel right.

Have anything stronger?

It's a bit early for gin, darling.

Never. Give me a hit off that joint.

I take a big inhale and hold it. It's shit.

Something's not right in my gut.

I need some air.

I step through the giant window and out onto the fire escape. There's a small weather-damaged chair and an ashtray filled with Benson & Hedges butts. I pick up a pack and look inside: a lighter and five smokes.

This is the kind of fucked-up situation in which I need a smoke. I light up. Menthol burns my throat. I can't feel any nicotine, just this burning pine taste in my throat. Like freebasing floor cleaner.

I'm facing other buildings that look familiar. It hits me. This is the building Oso lives in. I'm on top of all the drugs I could want. There's more black hole down there. That is, if I have my timing right. If this is when he's still alive.

I could fix this. I'm not risking anything. What's the worst that happens? I lose all my shit and end up in the psych ward? It's not that bad.

I stub out the cigarette and head back inside.

I need some clothes, I announce to no one in particular.

Go back in the room you slept in, Dallas says. *The closets in this place are full of old costumes and whatnot.*

The closet is jam-packed with all kinds of crazy shit. Feather boas, fake furs, real furs, gold lamé, some kind of disco-ball fabric I don't know the name of. Polyester, sharkskin, satin. I have no idea how to sort this shit out. I just throw it on the floor behind me as I dig.

I find a two-pieced denim thing. It looks like a leisure suit, but I think it will fit. It's long enough, but it's tight. Like a motherfucker. How thin were people in the '70s? I can't zip the pants up.

There's a kung fu outfit with drawstring pants. That'll do. Basically pajamas.

I'm fucked for shoes, though. There's nothing in here in my size. Not my style either, but that's beside the point. Holy hell, there are some ugly platforms and alligator disco boot things. I don't even know what these are called.

Dressed, I walk out into the hall, making sure I don't lock myself out. Winchell has turned every apartment on this floor into one big apartment. He's knocked out the walls between them. He's probably across the hall by himself at the moment. I'd check it out, but the pull of the drugs from downstairs is too strong.

I walk gingerly. You don't know what you're going to step on in this neighborhood. The carpet is dark and worn out. I think it used to be a burgundy color with some kind of pattern on it. I can see traces of what looks to be a flower shape along the edges of the hallway.

I skip the elevator and take the stairs. I go down one flight, then another. On the next flight, there's a slight familiar stink. Oso's floor.

I enter the hallway and follow my nose. It's the spot, all right. No doubt about it.

I knock, a shave-and-a-haircut knock.

Oso, homeboy, open up. It's Chuck.

No response.

I try the knob. Unlocked. I turn it and pull the door open.

There's a smell a man can make when shitting and pissing himself for days on end. It's a smell that nature uses to keep us away from the other sick animals. Only the most disgusting of predators will come near: the flies and the junkies.

Oso's lying on a futon mattress on the floor. The TV is on, blaring away true-crime shows that aren't nearly as bad as what I'm seeing. His hand twitches, and the channel changes to a hoarding show.

He's not dead. The resilience of drug addicts is phenomenal. They may want to die, but they won't until the drugs are ready to not be done any longer. The drugs will keep them alive so they can be done.

Part of me wants to call someone to get help for this insufferable condition, but there are two realities working against me. One: nothing is going to help this guy. Two: the drugs I need are inside him, and I must get them out.

I sit on Oso's chest and put my hands around his neck and squeeze. There's recognition in his eyes but no panic or anger. He'd lift his arms to get me off, but they're too heavy right now.

His neck is too big to get my hands around. It's slick with saliva and sweat and fuck knows what else. His skin swells with the strain of the marbles filling his pores.

I give up. I pick up a belt and put it around his neck. Slide one end through the buckle and pull tight. His face turns red. He struggles but fails. He's weighted down.

Unless I find a way out of this, this is what waits for me.

His torso ripples. His eyeball swells and pops like Bubble Wrap. Even with all this smell of shit and piss and death, the smell of the inside of an infected eyeball is still noticeable.

A giant black ball pops out and rolls across the floor. I was expecting more. But that one will do. It's the largest one I've seen, and it made a loud thump when it landed.

Oso is still. I killed him. Behind me, the TV flashes promos for one of those rednecks-with-money reality shows. It's the new version of *The Beverly Hillbillies*, and it's about as accurate. The worst thing you can do to poor people is dump a bunch of money on them. They'll kill themselves spending it like a fish that eats itself to death.

I pick up the marble. It's maybe too heavy to carry in a pocket.

My hands are disgusting. They're covered in Oso's death-goo.

I find the bathroom but notice right away something's different.

The bathtub is full of meth. Like one giant hunk of meth that's he's made. Holy fuck. It's a lot of meth. A lot. I wash my hands.

Think. I've been here before. There was a cookie tin of cocaine and a bunch of cash. It should be there.

I go in the kitchen, find a grocery bag. Cookie tin of coke. Check. Money, well, not as much as last time, but there's still a stack. Check. I find an ice pick and go back to the bathtub.

I'm hunking out what looks like a lifetime supply of meth and dropping it into the grocery bag when I hear the door. Fuck.

Someone is in the apartment. He screams when he sees Oso. *What the fuck? What happened to you?* he yells.

There are some more noises, followed by a disturbingly loud thump and agonizing screams.

If there's a chance, it's now, before anyone else shows up. I slip out the bathroom door and see Vietnam John, who has slipped on some goo-wet marbles and fallen on his knife. He's making a tourniquet out of the belt I left around Oso's neck.

I should run, but I freeze for a moment, and he sees me.

Chuck, you bastard, he says, *you did this. I'm going to cut you into one-inch cubes.*

I don't stick around to argue his point.

OLD NAVY

PAYLESS FOR SHOES. Done. Now for better clothes.

At the Old Navy on Market Street, I ask to get in the dressing room. The plan is get new clothes and wear them out of the store. Pay for them, of course, but I look like a real freak in these old costume clothes. And I can smell myself, and if you can smell yourself, everyone else smells you twice as much.

Chuck?

Fuck. Who is this? She's speaking to me like she's unsure. Like she's checking to make sure it's me.

It's Nancy. Nancy McKenna.

Nothing.

Nancy Suicide?

Oh shit. Nancy Suicide. God, I was so hot for her back in the day. Another hotshit punk girl who wouldn't give me the time of day. I talked to her at a few parties but never got any alone time with her. She always dated some foreign punk dude who showed up like some kind of fucking genie with an accent. As soon as one bailed out, another one took his place.

You look different. No dreadlocks.

Yeah, all corporate. Gotta pay the bills. What the fuck are you wearing?

Crazy night.

Smells like it. Hey, I don't mean to offend after all these years, but I can't have you funking up the clothes.

I'm going to buy them, I swear.

Are you sure? No offense, but you smell like you rolled in something dead.

Not too far from the truth.

Here. Go into booth three. Can I ask you something, and you promise you will take it in the spirit that it's intended?

For sure.

Um, I've been clean and sober for five years now, and it's been really great. I went back to school, got my teeth fixed . . .

I zone out. Not doing that bullshit. Don't need to hear it. Right now I need to do more drugs, not less. That shit is not going to help me. I nod and agree to something. I'm not sure if it's a Buddhist meditation or a Bible study or if she was trying to make amends; I really don't know and I don't care. I give her a number that used to be mine and head into the dressing room to change.

BACK TO WINCHELL'S

THERE'S ONLY SO many places you can go with cash and no ID and no credit cards. I can't get a hotel room. I can't rent that fucking party bus. There's nowhere to go but back to the Winchell apartment. I have to get one of them to get me that fucking party bus. It's my only link to when things were right.

When I walk in to Winchell's place, the old man is there. He looks two hundred years old but as mean as a snake. Some of those old theater queens are like old ladies at a retirement home, but some of them are the kind of fierce you earn from years of bitterness.

Who the fuck are you? he says with a sneer.

That's Chuck, the boy I was telling you about, Dallas says to calm him down.

I say nothing, but I walk to the table with my shopping bag. I take out the tin of cocaine and open it up. Nothing makes you more welcome than a cookie tin full of cocaine.

The old man snorts it up like a Shop-Vac. He's in good spirits.

Why, I haven't had any cocaine this good since the Reagan administration. Day that bastard took office, the street price of cocaine dropped three hundred percent. And it was good stuff, too, the kind of quality product that regular folks like you and I can't get a hold of.

He was a homophobic son of a bitch, that's for sure; didn't want to even say AIDS on TV. With a faggot son at that. That was one hot piece of ass, let me tell you. That boy whored it up in every queer neighborhood in America. Everyone wanted to fuck the president's kid. Who wouldn't? He had his pick of the litter. Liked those big-muscle fags, and I wasn't anywhere near that. Not even back then.

We all had great coke for about eight years, and then he went out of office and the quality dropped and everyone started doing meth instead. I was never into that stuff. Cocaine made me think everyone wanted to fuck me; meth made me think that everyone was hiding outside my window.

And when the drugs changed, the music changed. Disco had long died for the rest of the country, but it was still the official music of gay America. But meth killed disco and gave way to that bullshit house music. Ugh. Remember when gay people liked gay music? Donna Summer, Gloria Gaynor, and ABBA?

Don't get me started on the death of the musical. You know that's my thing. The strange part is that hip-hop kept me alive. Those talentless angels started sampling my work. I have points on dozens of rap records I've never listened to. Made more money from Jay-Z and Beyoncé than I ever did back in my heyday.

This is really good shit. I haven't had anything this good since my friend Bruce who used to be a limo driver for Bill Graham was still around. God I miss him. AIDS, of course, like everyone else who was beautiful. My only saving grace was being a plain Jane. Just didn't fuck enough to catch it. Bruce was a beautiful man who had an ass that looked like two cantaloupes in a pair of cutoff jeans.

Where did you find this? It makes me miss drugs. My generation's drugs. Quaaludes. Poppers. Real acid. That barrel-shaped-pill kind. Not that bullshit on paper. Orange sunshine. Now those were drugs.

You know what we should do? I say with my best Jack Nicholson coke grin. *We should get a party bus.*

Of course they agree with me. We're high out of our minds, and we have time, money, and yet more drugs. Winchell has a credit card and a clean DMV record, and I have cash and the drugs. It's perfect.

THE BUS

SAD MILES HOLDS a license to drive this thing. Turns out the man is a former muni driver. Makes sense, I suppose. Sad Miles. Sad-for-miles Miles, the bus driver. He doesn't look happy when he drives, but he looks a little more alive, like he has a purpose again.

Our little party grows at each stop. Harris orders stops at all his favorite bars, many of which no longer exist. Everyone who gets on is over sixty-five or under twenty-five.

The old ones are classic old queens from back in the day. Well dressed, biting senses of humor. Expensive but ordinary haircuts. No tattoos. They look like they stepped off a game show from 1972.

The young ones are like you'd expect. Perfect bodies. Eyes that light up with drugs the quality of which they've never had. Lots of cell phone pictures, themselves in every one, every picture a selfie. Their shirts come off quickly, and I don't blame them. I guess if they didn't look this good, Harris wouldn't have invited them on in the first place.

The bus is full. The music thumps. If there are twenty people on this bus, there are thirty conversations, coked-up plans and monologues and ideas, no one listening and everyone talking.

There are more drugs on here now than when we started. At some point, there will be less. At some point, there will be peak drugs, when we have the most drugs we're ever going to have here, bus or no bus. The smart party move is to bail out at that time and find a different scene. But I'm not here to party. I'm here to get high as fuck.

I get the marble out of my stash and look at it. The little black ball that started all my problems. It is my problem. Maybe it's the solution to my problems.

I smoke it. I fire it up and hit it again and again. I don't even give a fuck about being high anymore. I have to get back. I'm smoking with a sense of direction. Smoke it like it's the only way home.

The withdrawals hit as soon as I see him coming for me. The adrenaline rush doesn't help; I'm too sick for it to matter. The sidewalk is like ankle-deep wet mud. A crowd of Vietnamese ladies runs for the bus down the hill, opposite of me. I'm a drug-sick rock in the middle of a stream. I'm losing ground, being pushed backward. These women with their pink plastic bags mean business.

I see him closing in. A giant skinhead in the standard flight jacket. It's not a small jacket, but he's too big for anything. His head is a swirl of bloodless white and tempered red. His eyes are black buttons sewn into his face. A vein like a cable runs up the side of his neck and talons across his temple. I know he's coming for me.

I have a .25-caliber Raven in my pocket. This may be it. I'll have to wait till he gets right on me and empty the clip in his gut and run. I won't make it far. Even in the Tenderloin, you can't get away with this shit. I'm too sick to get away. I need money. I need my fix. Hell, I only really need my fix. That's the only reason I need money.

I've been here before. I've been here several times. Identical realties laid over one another like clear acetate sheets. This is where it always starts, isn't it? What came before this? What was I doing right before I got here?

Fearsweat soaks me. The sickness makes it worse. Everything's slowing to a stop. The world isn't going by at the same rate. Jones Street smells like dried and re-urinated-upon urine puddles, twice-peed stains in the cracks.

He gets closer, like frames are cut out of the movie. He's a slideshow of impending whatever it is he's going to do. I'm getting stomped, most likely. Kicked with steel-toed boots into submission and then ground down between heel and concrete. I'm mostly worried about my teeth being crushed. Everything else heals. Teeth are fucked forever.

I have to wait until he's close enough to read the tats on his neck. I have to grab him and jam this ridiculously small gun in one of the few soft spots he has—right underneath the sternum and between the top two ab muscles, these tiny lead pieces will take the fight right out of him. I'll take my chances with the law but not with this hulking monster.

The uphill sidewalk steepens. It looks like a fucking wall covered in cigarette butts and blacked circles of old gum. I can't move. Too sick.

I've been here before. Big Mike. It's okay. He'll help me.

Pinching on the arm. Grip so tight my fingers hurt. Ripping feeling in my shoulder. He turns me around, shoves me against a wall.

His eyes are full of blood and murder, two tiny black pinpricks into his soul built from failure.

He holds a sutured stump in my face that still smells of antiseptics.

I'm supposed to do something right here, at this moment; I'm always supposed to do something at this moment, and I never remember what it is. This is where my life begins.

I take out the twenty-five and shove it right in between his abs, notched for me to find by feel from hours of leg-raises and sit-ups. I squeeze the trigger, feel the firing pin strike the bullet.

Time stops.

ACKNOWLEDGMENTS

For starters, I should thank the influences you probably see: Philip K. Dick, William S. Burroughs, and Jim Carroll. I also should thank every single time-travel movie, from the shitty to the supreme, and also every questioning-reality film, from *eXistenZ* to *Jacob's Ladder*. All of these films have holes in them, but so do donuts, and you don't complain about the holes in those, you just enjoy the donut, right? If you take this book literally, it has problems, and so do you.

Okay, now on to some help you probably didn't know I had:

When I came to San Francisco in 1989, I picked up a copy of *Black Wheel of Anger* by Peter Plate. I read it three times in a row. I had never read anything like it. I later saw Peter read at a Food Not Bombs benefit. He had memorized his prose and recited it for everyone. Peter lived in a squat so he could spend time writing on a typewriter by candlelight in hours he would have otherwise spent working for rent money. What money he did have went to printing his books, which he gave away for free. He's San Francisco's most underrated writer, who writes love stories for the unlovable parts of the city; its gutters, alleys, and vacant lots; and the forgotten people who inhabit them.

There's a lot of Jon Longhi in this book. His four books of short stories inspired the anecdote-fueled fiction I write with here. His first collection, *Bricks and Anchors*, was in a regular rotation read, and I learned to write one- and two-page short stories from it, when the term "short-shorts" applied only to pants and not literature.

I'd like to thank Roberta, for watching this whole creative process while I was in the middle of a horrible cognitive meltdown; The Business, my weekly comedy show/partners, for giving me a consistent creative outlet and a safe place to write and create; Mick, for the weekly talks about art, the universe, and everything; my kettlebell friends from around the world that gave me rest from obsessing on a book; my Tuesday-night twelve-step crew, for reminding me that the dark moments always have a bit of humor; Bobcat, for a conversation about creativity and personal satisfaction he had with me that really lit a fire under my ass the more I thought about it; and Charlie Winton, for offhandedly mentioning he would like to look at a novel if I wrote one and for following through a long time later.

This book would not be possible without gentrification, which has been happening since I got here, but really, enough already. Pull it back a little. Slow it down. Please move to that plastic-bag island the size of Texas in the Pacific Ocean. I hear the weather is great and there's lots of parking.

This book would not be possible without the horribly failed War on Drugs, in which no one gives a fuck about the victims. I can score a bag of dope about a half an hour from where I type this, but it would take me two weeks or more to get into rehab. We would rather fill our prisons at greater expense than give people treatment for what really ails them.

I would like to thank every bullshit tweaker conspiracy I had to listen to while getting high; bad dreams I thought were warnings; misspelled tattoos; the massive misperceptions from detoxing; the overwhelming weirdness of the world on the third day without sleep; the delusions of grandeur Frankie Glitter Doll described after hours at the adult bookstore that sold used porn; the crow I saw eating a pigeon on Market Street; performance artists who stuck things up their asses in the name of any kind of statement; free poetry readings that were full of homeless savants and the mentally ill; the buses full of would-be artists, poets, and authors who came to San Francisco every summer and melted like snowmen in the harsh sunshine of cheap crank; punk bands that played loud in the warehouses of the Mission District and the cops who didn't give a shit; zine culture and glue sticks and those Kinko Keys that Dave stole; the Ghost of Frank's Depression that I swore was real; the smoking section at the Strand Theater; punk houses that always smelled like old socks and felt like home; the first dot-com era that now looks so small and naive compared to this one; the kindness of sex workers, ex-cons, and the insane who answered phone calls past midnight and were never shocked by anything I said; junkies who woke up stump-armed at SF General with nonconsensual amputations; bartenders that kept me after hours; and the donuts made in the twenty-fifth hour at the corner of Twentieth and Mission. I couldn't have done this without you.